THE CHIP MAKER

PROPHECY OF THE BEAST

BRIDGETTE L. COLLINS
WITH TERRY E. MCGEE SR.

THE CHIP MAKER
Published by Just In Time Publishing

ISBN: 978-0-9790932-4-1

Cover design by Brand Concepts Creative Media (770) 885-6486
Interior design and typeset by MagicGraphix.com

Printed in the United States of America.

For information:
JUST IN TIME PUBLISHING
P.O. Box 690032
Houston, Texas 77269

DEDICATION

This book is dedicated to Believers who will face the greatest test known to mankind.

CHAPTER 1

AUGUST 21, 2021

On the eve of accepting the highest award achievable in the world of technology, the owner of iTrack, Inc., and his supporters were poised to send an unprecedented message of compliance to individuals who refused to accept the device that had been created to advance their movement. The presentation of the award had been flaunted as a declaration of momentum, as well as a last chance for unsettled commitments. As the last in a chain of events designed to increase a spirit of fear drew near, it was a pivotal time for people who had failed to concede. The world was days away from a cascade of intentional events that would ultimately lead to the consolidation and centralization of numerous leadership powers into one; an anticipated prophecy of the system chosen to rule all mankind.

iTrack, Inc., had become known worldwide for its revolutionary enhancement of an implantable tracking device. Through its partnership with Global Media Sources, the world's largest media and entertainment conglomerate, iTrack used the company's communication infrastructure to plan and execute their movement, which would ultimately require every living being on Earth to acquire the implantable chip. At the root of the movement was the implementation of the *New World Access*, an agenda designed to facilitate a unified government, financial system, and religion for ease of the chosen system's control.

For years, Bible scholars had spoken about the progression of ethical deterioration in humanity, and many agreed the current conditions of humanity were symbolic of biblical prophecy signifying the nearing of end times. To further their movement, iTrack's owner and Global Media Sources' executives had used the ideas and discussions of Bible scholars to elevate panic and attract individuals with influential power to support and promote the *My Access Chip* movement.

The time for public praise was hours away. On Sunday, August 22, 2021, *The Washington Post* would hold its prestigious recognition ceremony at The Kennedy Multicultural Center in South Dallas, Texas. David Denmart, chairman and CEO of Global Media Sources, would stand alongside Jim Natas, the owner of iTrack, as he received *The Washington Post*'s Trumpet Award for the company's visionary enhancement of the implantable tracking device.

Saturday morning, August 21, 2021, in Dallas, Texas, started out at 85 degrees, with the sun gradually piercing through the clouds around eight o'clock. On the north side of Dallas, Larry Shepherd, a top executive for Global Media Sources, stood on the greens of Country Creek Golf Club, on the seventh hole, along with his boss, Matt Meyers, President of Global Media Sources, and Sam Walker, the Chief of Security. Larry was getting ready to play one of the toughest holes on the course.

"My pastor will be attending the recognition ceremony tomorrow night," Larry said with a hearty smile, trying to distract his fellow golfers.

The hole included three small hills, numerous trees, green grass, a stone teeing ground, and a yardage sign.

"I'm glad to hear that. Pastor Dobbs and many other pastors were instrumental in helping us market and gain support of Project My Access Chip," Mr. Meyers replied as he motioned for Sam to hand him his favorite driver.

"They were definitely instrumental in helping dispel the conspiracy theory of our anti-supporters, like Pastor McFarland," Sam said, "and his stir about the Antichrist, Mark of the Beast and Chosen One."

"With his messages targeting the hopeless, Pastor Dobbs' influence, along with our strategic instruments of persuasion, have attracted masses of dejected, rejected, neglected, lonely, and unhappy people to hop on the My Access Chip train," Mr. Meyers gloated.

"Right! The hopeless," Sam agreed.

"Miserable, unhappy people who lack control over their lives, love to complain, blame, and join forces with others who share their same sentiments about life and the plot to mistreat them."

Larry laughed.

"Those same unhappy people are willing to do anything to get — for free — what they believe society owes them," Sam commented.

"We can get people every time with the freebies," Mr. Meyers blurted out in a jovial tone.

"Our plan to provide free business loans, free federal loan forgiveness, free health care insurance, free college, and other enticing free programs really helped us get more and more people chipped," Larry stated.

"Yes, you and your team did a great job creating and promoting those programs through our various advertising platforms and social media forums. The words 'provide' and 'free' were synonymous with 'get chipped,'" Mr. Meyers emphasized.

Larry smiled. "And, that youngster, Stanley, was a good hire. With his ingenious mind, he was able to create a plethora of messages on our social networking tools, iAccessagram, iAccessBook, and iAccessBlog, to inform, educate, and foster support of getting chipped."

"And recruit radical minds, namely those seeking fame and glory," Sam added.

Larry shook his head and exclaimed, "Yes, his ingenious ways of attracting and gaining followers on social media were simply brilliant."

"I still don't know how he created so many fake social media accounts," Sam said.

"Yes, fake accounts that connected friends," Larry shared. "Then the messages he created to disseminate information and ultimately recruit those radical minds helped us increase our level of fear tactics."

"And establish a new normal of domestic militants," Sam interjected.

"Yes, the SAVERS group has quite a following," Larry acknowledged.

"Don't forget, we've also benefitted from all the recent catastrophes and pandemic arousals," Mr. Meyers said.

"Yes, those planned and unplanned," Sam said with a smile.

Mr. Meyers shot Larry an unremorseful glance and said, "Indeed, the execution of targeted suicide bombings, mass shootings, plane crashes, train derailments, civilian attacks, kidnappings, along with the calculated death of Senator Ryan Paul Patrick helped us gain another million implants."

Sam looked at Larry and asked, "What about the bombing scheduled for this morning?"

"Done. I received a text message earlier," Larry confirmed. "While we're here, emergency personnel are responding and attending to many injuries, which include fatalities at the park. Our reporters are in the studio and on the ground. Jenny Purdue, Martin Matthews, Matt Nicholas, and the like are all earning those half-million dollar salaries this morning. Social media is blowing up the Internet community as we speak."

"And next on the list?"

"Other planned attacks are underway for this weekend at a couple of the remaining pre-season football games, jazz festivals, end of summer festivities, and back to school events. The hurricane brewing in the Gulf should also generate a number of deaths. People won't know if their family members and friends are alive or dead. More fear to get chipped," Larry said as he nodded with assurance.

"And our new administration's help with perpetuating the overseas wars has helped generate a lot of civilian and military deaths — not to mention our foreign partners' threat of nuclear weapons ready to be launched. All well worth the two trillion dollars we've contributed on several fronts," Mr. Meyers said.

"Definitely so, sir," Larry responded.

Mr. Meyers smiled and asked, "What about the accident?"

"Done," Larry assured. "Both Cho's wife and daughter are fighting for their lives at Mercy Methodist Hospital."

"What about the disappearance?"

"Mo Money Monte's mother is being held at a secret location and will be discarded if he doesn't comply."

"Great!" Mr. Meyers nodded. "I expect he will comply and announce his endorsement of the chip tomorrow night."

"Pastor McFarland's *Wake Up Call* event never should have happened. But since it did, it'll teach those with intentions to incite controversy about the chip that there are consequences."

"Unfortunate for those who support his message of waking people up to recognize the so-called delusion of the chip. They'll suffer an unwarranted death."

Larry looked ahead. "There are still many who are running away."

Mr. Meyers abruptly cut him off, looking sternly at him as he said, "It's mandatory. There will be severe consequences for those who remain without it. There will be no hiding places. The *Pledge* is for real, and those who don't take it will surely die."

The *Pledge* had become Global Media Sources' signature campaign for gaining visibility and promoting the *My Access Chip* as a necessary device. The goal was to get people to show their support for the chip by taking the pledge and agreeing to acquire the implantable chip. On the surface, the campaign was the Organizers' (an elite group of chip supporters and promoters) way of instilling in individuals the idea of necessary identification, easy access living, and safety.

"And for individuals receiving governmental assistance, the mandatory requirement for them to get chipped as a part of being compliant with the continuing receipt of their benefits has been monumental," Larry said. The requirement was part of a greater movement working behind the scenes.

Mr. Meyers removed his sunglasses and said, "Our goal is to have every living human organism chipped. Jim Natas is the owner of iTrack. His chip is the core of control."

Larry inhaled deeply and shook his head in agreement. "The hunt for my wife, kids, and her mother is still on."

Larry's wife, mother-in-law, and three kids, ages five, ten, and twelve, had been missing for two months.

"What exactly is our team doing to find them?" Mr. Meyers demanded. "Sam has their descriptions, right? What are they using for money?"

"I know Sam and his team are scouring the city and residences of distance relatives, but nothing yet," Larry said softly, looking at Sam. "My wife had become so paranoid towards me because I insisted it was time for her and the kids to get the chip."

"It's imperative their disappearance remains a secret," Mr. Meyers said sternly. "Since you're so close to the movement, we don't know who all is involved in their disappearance and what information your wife may have shared."

"She still hasn't tried to contact your pastor or any of your church members?" Sam asked.

"No. She'd become wary of Pastor Dobbs, so I know she wouldn't contact him."

Practicing his swing back and forth, Mr. Meyers let out a soft "Hmm." His movements were slow and edgy.

Nervous, Larry began to wipe sweat from his forehead, then quickly said, "I discreetly asked a couple of the ladies in the Women's Ministry if she'd contacted them, but no one has heard from her. Basically, I just acted surprised that she hadn't contacted them to find out the happenings at our church. For the most part, I just told folks she's visiting some of her mom's relatives in New Jersey."

Mr. Meyers handed his golf club back to Sam, then glanced at his watch, noticeably agitated, and said, "It's been two months."

As the impact of the disappearance sank in, Larry and Sam turned to stare at each other. They reeked of a probing anxiety.

"I know, sir." Larry breathed in deeply and nodded.

Mr. Meyers sneezed and said, "At the top of my list of irritants is a man who can't control his household. The ability to do so, or not, is an example of his influence, persuasion, and leadership ability."

"Bless you, sir," Larry said quickly.

"Bless you, sir," Sam interjected.

Larry hurriedly placed his golf ball on the rubber tee as Sam looked down at his handheld GPS.

"Why is it so hard for our top-notch security team to find a woman, three kids, and a demented old lady?" Mr. Meyers snapped, staring at Sam. He was frustrated that such a dangerous loose end existed, one that potentially had access to secret information.

Sam placed his GPS device in his bag and looked at the parade of cars entering and exiting the golf center building.

"Well?" Mr. Meyers said, glaring at Sam with contempt.

"It's like they've gone underground. Vanished," Larry said. "But I'm confident the private investigators Sam has hired will find them."

"Sam, I want to hear your solution!" demanded Mr. Meyers.

"We're on it, Boss," Sam replied swiftly.

"A better question would be, how can I be sure about the proficiency of our next actions?" Mr. Meyers snapped.

Sam glanced over at Larry, then back at Mr. Meyers. "Sir, they'll go off as scheduled, without a hitch."

After a moment of tense silence, Larry said with assurance, "Our initiatives have been very fruitful over the past eight months. More than five billion people have been chipped throughout the world. We still have significant ground to cover, but at least we're right upon the light at the end of the tunnel."

"Yes, we still have significant ground to cover. We haven't met our goal," Mr. Meyers retorted.

"The support of the new White House administration has been very helpful," Larry added.

Mr. Meyers boasted, "Definitely so. We contributed a lot of money and resources to ensure our candidate was elected, but I'm not happy about the fact that we haven't met our goal."

"The benefits and requirements of the free government programs will continue to be a key factor in boosting the numbers," Sam chimed in.

"Yes, many people have taken advantage of the free Education Program, Small Business Program, Social Security Disability Program, and other programs. But we haven't met our goal," Mr. Meyers reiterated.

"Sir, with a coalition of domestic and international attacks scheduled, I guarantee you we'll meet our goal by the end of this month," Larry promised.

"Today is August 21st!" Mr. Meyers shouted.

"Yes, sir," Larry responded.

Mr. Meyers hollered, "With a current world population of approximately 7.8 billion, we are nowhere close to this number — and our mandatory time period to have everyone chipped is this month! Plus, we have loose ends!"

Sam placed his hand on Mr. Meyers' shoulder and said, "Boss, too much is at stake. We'll reach our goal. I assure you. With the strategic devastation plans in progress, we'll reach our goal. People will be running to their nearby hospitals, clinics, and other designated locations begging to get chipped."

Mr. Meyers looked over at Larry. "Denmart and Natas will be in town later this afternoon. I don't want them having any concerns or doubts about the movement and the goal when they're speaking at the podium tomorrow evening during the recognition ceremony. And Larry's family will be found and discarded along with the others who are assisting them. They all will be treated like lost sheep to be slaughtered."

Sam quickly redirected Mr. Meyers' attention to their golf game.

"Okay, Larry, it's time to stop delaying the game." Sam started to whistle as he motioned with his hand, a cheeky grin on his face. He said, "Tough shot for an amateur."

As Larry began to line up his shot, the cloudy blue skies suddenly turned to darkness. The men then heard the deafening sound of a trumpet as the earth underneath them started to tremble.

"What's happening?" Larry shouted, sounding like a scared child.

"Run!" Mr. Meyers shouted with panic.

"Don't run," Sam said while bracing his feet. "Just stay calm. Drop down on the ground."

"Stay calm?!" Mr. Meyers yelled out. "The ground is moving!"

"Everyone, drop down and cover your head and neck with your hands and arms," Sam said.

Dust filled the air while the men proceeded to fall to the ground on their hands and knees. Others on the course started to run hysterically across the shaking, manicured lawn, heading toward the golf club center, but they fell to the ground before reaching the building.

"It's probably just some seismic activity!" Sam shouted as he placed his hand on Mr. Meyers' shoulder.

"In Texas?! Everyone is running towards the building!" Larry shouted as he covered his head. "It's too late to run. Out here in the clear is the best place to be."

Seconds later, cars were trying to speed out of the country club's parking lot. People were screaming, tires were screeching, and cars were swiftly caught up in a traffic jam above the shaking earth. Larry, Mr. Meyers, and Sam raised their heads as the scene unfolded in front of them and the disturbing commotion became increasingly bizarre: before their eyes, people around them started to vanish.

Samuel Cho, an ex-Global Media Sources employee, was across town at Mercy Methodist Hospital in Rockwall, Texas, sitting next to his wife's hospital bed. His wife, Malin, and daughter, Adrika, had been involved in a ten-car collision. On the way home from the *Wake Up Call* event at their church, an 18-wheeler truck hit the Ford Explorer his wife was driving on Interstate 30. The collision sent their vehicle flying through the air, hitting a highway retainer wall before coming to rest on its side. Cars swerving all around them had caused multiple crashes and resulted in massive injuries. Two fatalities had caused the shutdown of the freeway for several hours. His wife still lay in a coma, while his daughter was in another hospital room. The doctors had informed Cho that his daughter was paralyzed from the neck down.

Cho's face reflected an unresolved peace and confidence as he spoke to God about his wife. On his knees with his eyes closed, he said, "God, You know how much I love my wife. Please let her wake up. Give her more time on Earth. There is so much more work for the two of us to do together. I need her, but above all, our daughter Adrika needs her mother. Please. Please. Please, let her wake up. We have so much to complete on our journey. I know her lying here is a part of Your plan, but please let her wake up! I love her so much!"

Pastor McFarland entered the hospital room. He stood silently, watching Cho.

After a few moments, Pastor McFarland cleared his throat, and Cho turned around and stood up, with tears in his eyes.

"Hi, Pastor," he greeted him. Pastor McFarland embraced Cho. "Thank you for coming back," he said, happy to see his pastor. "Have a seat."

Pastor McFarland dragged a nearby chair and positioned it beside Cho's chair, then he and Cho both sat down next to Malin's bed.

"I wanted to stop by on my way to the conference and see if there were any changes throughout the night. Glad they allowed me in before visiting hours. How's she doing?"

"Among her many injuries is a fractured skull. The doctors say she has fluid on her brain as a result of the impact of the accident. After the emergency eight-hour surgery, the doctors say it's just wait-and-see right now. She could be in the coma for four days, four months, four years, or permanently."

"Everyone at church knows about the accident and is praying for her and Adrika."

"It's a mystery to me the airbags in the car didn't work."

"I'm sure the police department will conduct an investigation."

"Are you thinking foul play, too?"

"They just need to investigate whether the airbags were deliberately tampered with or defective."

"I took the vehicle in for an inspection just yesterday. Everything was fine. The service took longer than usual, but they noted everything as being fine."

Pastor McFarland nodded attentively, looking at Cho. He remained quiet, not wanting to say anything that would stress him further.

"It hasn't even been twenty-four hours since the accident, and they're already asking me about donating her organs!" Cho exclaimed.

Pastor McFarland began to look at Malin, lying in her hospital bed. Scanning her visible bruises, wounds, and the various intensive care equipment connected to her body, he thought about her recovery. From the intravenous tube, respirator/ventilator and other equipment, he knew what she needed most was prayer.

"With all that's happened to us, Pastor McFarland, I'm beginning to question God."

"That's a normal reaction," the pastor replied. "But you know and feel God's presence is in this place. He has your wife and daughter in His hands."

"I know, Pastor."

"I want to take this opportunity to pray for Malin and Adrika. Let us pray."

Clinching his chair with both hands, Cho closed his eyes and bowed his head. Pastor McFarland took Cho's hands, then he began to pray.

"Glorious Father, we come today thanking You for Your love and compassion. We thank You for Your peace and strength, and for giving us a sound mind in times of uncertainty, fear, and weakness. All powerful Father, please let Your ears be considerate to our prayers. Holy Spirit, we ask You to replace uncertainty, fear, and weakness with victory and praise. Triumphant Lord, You are the Alpha and Omega, the beginning and the end. Only You can raise Malin and Adrika up from their current state. Sovereign Lord, only You know the outcome. Whatever it may be, we will continue to praise You, honor You, and give You all of the glory. In Jesus' name. Amen."

"Thank you, Pastor."

"Everything will work out according to God's plan and purpose."

Cho stood and said, "I know." He moved closer toward Malin and listened intently to the sound of the machines keeping her still body at functioning capacity. With watery eyes, he looked at Pastor McFarland and said, "I need to visit my daughter."

"Don't worry about your daughter. My wife is with her right now."

"She's tough, you know," Cho said proudly.

"Yes, I know."

"She's been through so much. More than any young person should have to endure," Cho said, his face beginning to wrinkle.

"Remember, God is here. He's in control. His will shall be done," Pastor McFarland said in an encouraging tone.

"It's hard for me to believe the accident wasn't deliberate," Cho said.

"I know."

"With all the pressure and subtle threats to get the chip..." Cho stopped mid-sentence.

"The Pledge," Pastor McFarland said.

"Yes, the Pledge," Cho confirmed, "and those who don't support the Pledge."

"Now isn't the time to think about that."

Cho's temperament was one of quiet strain. He said softly, "I know this is their way of punishing me. First, my termination from Global Media for speaking out with you on TV against what they're trying to do, and now the accident that has both my wife and daughter here. I believe it goes back even further, to the destruction of my company, which caused my daughter to be burned over 50% of her body."

"Now isn't the time to think about those things," Pastor McFarland said again. "All we can do is speculate right now. Thinking your connection to me made things worse for you and your family, that's not important now. The healing and recovery of your wife and daughter is what we need to focus our attention on at this time."

"Thank you, Pastor!" Cho said, a bit encouraged. Pastor McFarland smiled. "The doctor will probably be back shortly. I need to get some air and go see Adrika. Can you stay with Malin until I return?" Cho asked.

"Sure, I will."

Cho leaned towards Malin's face and kissed her on the cheek. As Pastor McFarland turned around to sit down, the door opened; it was Malin's nurse with a flower arrangement in her hands.

"Mr. Cho, these were brought to our nurses' station for your wife," the nurse said as she placed the arrangement on top of Malin's bed tray stand.

Cho saw a card and pulled it out of the arrangement, then read the message on the card aloud. "Your former family at Global Media Sources would like to express its deepest sentiments for what has happened to your wife and daughter. You and your family are in our thoughts and prayers. If you need us, don't hesitate to contact us."

Cho threw the card and floral stick in the trash can. Shocked and troubled, he looked at Pastor McFarland, then stormed out of the room, nearly knocking over a patient in the hallway who was rolling his IV stand.

The nurse looked at Pastor McFarland and asked, "Is everything okay?"

Pastor McFarland looked uncomfortable as he said, "Everything will be okay."

Sitting in his car, Cho began to talk to the Lord.

"Lord, I've been a good and faithful servant. I attend church regularly. I treat people with love, kindness, and the utmost respect! I spoke out against the wrongdoings at Global Media Sources and sacrificed the safety of my family to expose their mission and how they plan to control the world. I know they've been after me for months, and I knew my life would be in danger as they tried to force me and my family to get that chip. Through it all, I've remained faithful and steadfast in my trust of You, Lord, knowing they were behind the destruction of my company, and now the freeway accident that has my wife and daughter fighting for their lives. I've been a good servant, Lord! Please heal my wife and daughter."

With his head bowed, it seemed as if Cho could hear God audibly saying, "Yes, *you've been a good and faithful servant. When I allowed the storms, you never turned away from Me! Even now, in the midst of those who seek to destroy you through your family because you will not succumb to their wishes and demands, you seek Me more, not less! And eternal life with Me is the prize you have earned! Now lift your head and join Me and your brothers and sisters!*"

As Cho lifted his head, he heard the sound of a trumpet. Looking through his windshield, he noticed the sky was very different and a reverse funnel cloud was spinning. People driving cars who were entering the hospital parking area stopped suddenly, and he heard tires screaming over the piercing horns of the other cars.

Moments later, Cho vanished.

Mo Money Monte, slim and strong-looking, wearing loafers and a blazer, stood in the foyer of his mother's house with Officer Smith, a short and stocky, sharp-eyed young officer who had been sent to the home of Mo Money Monte's mother in response to a missing persons report.

"You're Mo Money Monte, the rapper! I bet you're glad to be out of prison," Officer Smith exclaimed. "Any new music coming out soon?"

"Officer, my mother is missing," Mo Money Monte said with a purposefully controlled calm.

"I'm thinking my brother, House Representative Tadd Smith, had something to do with your release earlier this year. I heard you were supposed to be a part of that concert tour with Bone Esquire," the officer continued.

Startled by the extent of his statements, Mo Money Monte gathered his composure and said loudly, "Officer, I made the 911 call because my mother is missing!"

"What makes you think your mother is missing?" Officer Smith asked with his eyebrows raised and a half-smile, trying to agitate Mo Money Monte's noticeable distress.

"The last time I saw her was last night, after I brought her home from a conference at our church."

"What's the name of your church?"

"Triumphant Baptist Church."

"Isn't Stewart McFarland the pastor there?"

"Yes, he is."

The officer took a notepad from the pouch of his belt. "What time did you last see her?"

"It was around nine o'clock when I dropped her off here."

"Did you go inside with her?"

"Normally, I would have. But she told me she'd be okay, so I watched her go inside and left."

"Don't we love how our mothers are always concerned about our welfare?" Officer Smith said as he opened the notepad to a clean piece of paper and started to write. "Did you see any cars on the street when you dropped her off?" he continued.

"Officer Smith, I wasn't paying any attention to cars on the street! This is a neighborhood. People park cars on the street all day!"

"So again, what makes you think she's missing?"

"I was scheduled to pick her up this morning for the second day of the conference. I called to find out how soon she'd be ready, but she didn't answer. So, I came over. Except my mother isn't here. And that's her car in the driveway."

Mo Money Monte pointed to the black 2020 Lincoln SUV in his mother's driveway.

"You know our mothers will skip out in a heartbeat to catch a sale. Maybe she's with one of her friends," Officer Smith said.

"Not my mother, Officer."

"Is there anything out of order in the house?" Mo Money Monte frowned but said nothing. "Has anything been disturbed, Mr. Money Monte?"

"As far as I can tell, everything is in order."

"Maybe she's at the grocery store, having breakfast, or getting coffee somewhere with a friend."

"I've called and called her. It's not like her not to answer her cell phone."

"Have you checked with other family members and friends?"

"Yes, I have."

"What's your mother's name?"

"Irene Mascot."

"What's her physical description?"

"She's Caucasian, fifty-eight, around five-feet-four inches, with hazel eyes and brown hair."

Officer Smith grimaced as he wrote down the information. "Guess you get your color from whoever your dad is."

"What did you say?" Mo Money Monte snapped.

Officer Smith quickly asked his next question. "Do you know what she was last wearing?"

"Yes, she was wearing a black dress suit with a black hat trimmed with a rich mix of beads, sequins, and rhinestones."

"Sounds like a pretty fancy hat."

"Yes. Those are the sort of hats my mother wears."

"Does your mother have the *My Access Chip*?" Officer Smith asked.

Mo Money Monte began to speak sharply and said sternly, "No, she doesn't, Officer Smith."

"Well, if she had it, it sure could tell us where she's at right now. But for now, if she doesn't return home, you can file a report after she's been missing twenty-four hours."

Shaking his head, Mo Money Monte looked at the officer and said, "Man, my mother is missing. I need for you to issue whatever you folks issue so she can be found."

Seconds later, an attractive, sophisticated lady appeared in the doorway and asked, "Honey, is everything okay?"

Mo Money Monte said, "The good officer was just telling me I have to wait twenty-four hours before I can report my mother missing."

"Good morning, ma'am," Officer Smith said, acknowledging her presence.

"Hi, Officer. I'm Pamela Hobbs. As you can imagine, he's upset, not knowing the whereabouts of his mother."

"I know, Ms. Hobbs, but there's nothing we can do right now."

As Mo Money Monte let out a huge sigh, Officer Smith retrieved one of his cards from his uniform pocket and said sarcastically, "Mr. Mo Money Monte, here's my card. If the need to report her missing arises, just call me."

"For the record, I've reverted back to my biological name of Ivan Shepherd," Mo Money Monte said.

With a look of contempt, Officer Smith said, "I heard," then turned and walked away.

As Mo Money Monte walked back inside with Pamela, shaking his head, he said, "Guess who his brother is?"

"Who?"

"House Representative Tadd Smith!"

"The Tadd Smith endorsing the Pledge?"

"Absolutely!"

"Wow! What a coincidence," Pamela said.

"A coincidence maybe. Maybe not."

Mo Money Monte grabbed Pamela's hand and said, "Do you know what he asked me?"

"What?"

"He wanted to know if my mother was chipped."

"The pressure is on, Ivan. The subliminal messages are being moved more and more to the forefront. On I-20 the other day, I saw a billboard that said, 'How far will you go to protect you and your loved ones? Take the Pledge. Get chipped'!"

"They're popping up all over the place!"

"I know. It's scary, Ivan!"

"Don't worry, we have a higher protection."

"What are we going to do?"

"For starters, Bone! I know his involvement and my non-participation with the Pledge Concert has something to do with my mother's disappearance."

"You think?" Pamela inquired.

"Yes!" he shouted out. "I'm going to see him."

"Do you want me to call my sister, Jasmine, and find out if she knows anything? As an insider with Global Media Sources, she could find out some things for us."

"No, I don't want to involve her. These people will utilize whatever means necessary to make a point, and I don't want her to become a target. They're probably watching her anyway since you're her sister and you're connected to me."

"Okay."

"In case something happens to me, I'm on my way to Bone Esquire's recording studio on Maple Ave." Mo Money Monte took a pad from a table drawer in the foyer and began to write. "Here's the address to his office," he said, handing Pamela a piece of paper. "I know my defiance has something to do with my mom's disappearance."

Mo Money Monte kissed Pamela on her forehead and rushed out the front door, and she stood on the porch and watched him get into his car. As he drove away, she dialed a number on her cell phone.

At the sound of a voice on the other end, she said in a mysterious tone, "He just left."

Bone Esquire's recording studio was located in Dallas' upscale Uptown Park area. Mo Money Monte entered the building in a state of panic. He was quickly greeted at the entrance doors by two female bodyguards dressed in black tailor-made suits. The beautiful, chiseled looking women were a picturesque vision in their high heels, with their pistols visibly showing in soft leather holsters.

"I'm here to see Bone."

"You're Mo Money Monte?" asked one of the guards.

"That's my old name. I go by Ivan Shepherd now."

One of the female bodyguards pointed to the nearby elevators and said, "Take the elevator to the 15th floor."

As Mo Money Monte exited the elevator, another female bodyguard greeted him.

"Mo Money Monte?" she asked.

Mo Money Monte frowned and said, "Yes. But I've reverted to my birth name of Ivan Shepherd. Please address me as Ivan Shepherd."

"Mr. Esquire is expecting you. Please wait here."

Mo Money Monte scanned the framed pictures of various artists and framed platinum records that adorned the walls of the lobby area; memories dating back to their years as breakout artists and signing with their first major record label. Reflections of their nominations for best record, album, song and new artist started to roam through his mind. Seconds later, Bone appeared.

"What's up, Mo!"

"I understand you're expecting me."

"Yes, I am. Come on back," Bone said.

Bone Esquire led the way toward his office, and Mo Money Monte started to follow. As they walked down the hall, two different muscular women dressed in black suits appeared behind them. Disturbed and puzzled, Mo Money Monte continued following Bone Esquire with the two women trailing behind them.

Entering Bone's office, Mo Money Monte shouted out, "I know you had something to do with my mother's disappearance!"

"Mo, come on, man! Your mother? Really?!"

"Bone, we're talking about my mom. If you had anything to do with my mother's disappearance, I swear you're a dead man."

Bone quickly interrupted, smiling, and said, "Um, so much for your Christian walk. Dead man...really?"

"Where is my mother?" Mo Money Monte shouted as he lunged towards Bone.

"Calm down. Calm down. Violent acts don't solve anything," Bone said with a smile.

Before he could reach Bone, the two women grabbed Mo Money Monte's arms and restrained him. Bone then reached in his desk and retrieved a large manila envelope.

"Oh, how I remember those Sunday soul food meals your mother would cook. Southern deep fried chicken, black-eyed peas, collard greens, corn bread and sweet potato pie. I'll never forgot the time she served barbecued ribs, cabbage, macaroni and cheese and banana pudding for dessert. Um um good! It was right before you went to prison."

He extended the envelope toward Mo Money Monte, and the women released him so he could accept it.

"What is this?"

"Open it, and you'll see."

Mo Money Monte yanked the envelope and opened it. He then pulled out a document and began to flip through the pages.

"Read it!" Bone snapped.

"What is this?" Mo Money Monte asked.

"What does it look like?"

"It looks like some sort of contract," Mo Money Monte said with a frown.

"Yes, a contract you need to sign if you want to see your darling mother again. Your time is up!" Bone said as an enormous stab of pain went through Mo Money Monte's face. "You see, you *will* get chipped, and you *will* be a part of *The Pledge Access Concert Tour* — or your mother *will* surely die."

Holding the document, Mo Money Monte stared blankly at it.

"I sure hate it had to come to this," Bone continued. "When the Organizers want something, they want it. I don't need you to pull off this tour, but they want you involved. Despite the crowds I've been pulling for the past couple months, they believe your influence, combined with mine, will have a greater impact in manipulating all our followers to get chipped. The reign of our chosen system and millions and millions of dollars are at stake. There's a celebratory dinner tomorrow night at the Executive Mansion. If you want to see your mother again, you'll be at the dinner and ready to announce your endorsement of the chip. Plus, we'll have a doctor there to chip you live as part of our promotional campaign. You'll dispute the rumors and say your intent was not to hold out, but to get chipped publically at this event. As you're getting chipped, hundreds of Pledge supporters will be across town at The Kennedy Multicultural Center, where Mr. Denmart will share the stage with Mr. Natas as he receives *The Washington Post*'s Trumpet Award. During the event, they'll spotlight *The Pledge Access Concert*, your involvement, and our tour dates."

Barely listening to Bone, Mo Money Monte continued to stare at the document. "Where is my mother?!" he shouted.

"Don't worry. She's in a safe place for now," Bone said, laughing loudly as Mo Money Monte stood paralyzed. "Just so there's no lack of communication about the opposition, Pastor McFarland and his followers will be dealt with for their antics against the movement," Bone said calmly. "Be glad the Organizers believe you're more valuable alive than dead. This is your only option for keeping your mother alive. In my opinion, it would have been easier to just kill you off with the others."

Standing horrified, Mo Money Monte was completely helpless; he didn't want to say or do anything that would promote greater risk for his mother. With his head bowed down, Mo Money Monte suddenly felt a warm sensation starting to travel throughout his body. The flooring in the office started to rumble, and the furnishings in Bone's office started shaking. Mo

Money Monte fell back into a chair as Bone grabbed hold of his desk. Objects fell on the floor, and the two women grabbed Mo Money Monte's arms to pull him up. They could hear people outside Bone's office yelling. They all staggered into the hallway and saw staff members in a frenzy, trying to make their way to the emergency exit doors.

The sound of a trumpet blasted through the office walls. With the shaking of the building, everyone inside could feel the earth starting to move underneath the building.

"Man, let's move! We've gotta get outta here!" Bone shouted in a terror-stricken tone, looking back at Mo Money Monte and the two women.

Moments later, Mo Money Monte vanished.

Chasity, the twenty-something daughter of Mr. Meyers, had summoned Luke, the young production assistant at Global Media Sources, to come over to her luxury apartment in Turtle Creek Estates. She'd lured him over with a message that she wanted to share some important breaking news. Standing in front of Chasity's front door, Luke began to knock softly. Getting no answer, he knocked harder and yelled out her name.

The door opened, and Chasity stood there, barely clothed in her robe and slippers.

"Yelling? Really, Luke?!" Chasity said. "I just got out of the shower."

Luke stood silent, looking at the silhouette of her shapely body underneath her robe.

"Well, don't just stand there. Come in."

As they entered her apartment, Chasity urgently began to pull Luke through her entrance hallway.

Before reaching her living room area, Luke stopped her and asked, "What's so important?"

Chasity turned and excitedly hugged him tight with sudden enthusiasm. "Don't you look nice in your church clothes, Church Boy. On your way to that *Wake Up Call* event?"

Luke ignored her comment, wiggled out of her embrace, and continued walking.

As she walked behind him, Chasity whispered in his ear, "I'm just wondering…under that nice suit, what lies? Is there a chip yet?"

His face turned to a strain, and he whispered softly in her ear, "No."

"Luke, Daddy has warned you. Non-chip bearers will surely die!"

Luke responded forcibly, "Like I said, NO, Chasity! I haven't, and I'm not going to."

"Come on in and have a seat, Church Boy," Chasity said as she walked in front of him. "Help me fold some clothes."

"Chasity, I'm on my way to the conference! I don't have time to help you fold clothes."

"Come on, Luke."

"Chasity, I know this isn't why you called me over here," Luke said, looking bewildered. "If you think you're going to convince me to do something I know I'm not going to do, you're sadly mistaken."

"Sit!"

Luke made a face as he looked at the two laundry baskets piled high with clothes in front of him on the sofa table.

Chasity sat down alongside Luke and said, "It's really sad about those runners."

"What runners?" Luke said.

"Haven't you heard the news?"

With a nervous stare, Luke asked, "What news?"

"Were you at the park running this morning?" Chasity said with a questioning look. She knew Luke typically ran his long distance miles on Saturday mornings.

"Yes!"

"There was a suicide bomber there this morning," Chasity said as she continued to be evasive.

"What are you talking about? I ran sixteen miles at the park this morning with hundreds of other runners, and everything was fine when I left to go home."

"Are you sure everything was okay?"

"No, I'm not sure, but…"

Chasity placed her hand on his leg and said, "Umm."

"I need to get to church! So what are you talking about?" Luke said. He was becoming annoyed with Chasity and her insinuations.

"Okay. I received a call about the news report of a man running in the park dressed in an Army combat uniform. Jenny and Matthew are at the TV studio talking about it now."

She started to hand Luke some towels to fold.

"Yes, I did see him towards the end of my run. I got to the park around five o'clock this morning," Luke said as he took a towel and began to fold it. "I remember he had on the traditional tan, gray and green camouflage Army attire, with the matching hat and Army combat boots. I remember him having a large camouflage field pack. Thinking he was so patriotic."

"Field pack?" Chasity questioned.

"Yes, field pack. Backpack. Whichever you prefer to call it. I just know it looked like it weighed a ton, and I thought, *He's running with all of that on?* True soldier."

Luke's look of concern heightened as Chasity stood up and went towards her television.

"I know you listen to satellite gospel in your car, so you probably haven't heard or seen the news," Chasity said as she picked up the TV remote.

Abruptly cutting her off, Luke said, "What news, Chasity?! What are you playing around about? Just say what you want to say. I've got to get to church."

"I'm just glad you got out in time," Chasity said.

"In time for what?"

Just as Chasity was getting ready to turn on her TV to reveal what she wanted to tell Luke, the sound of a large boom erupted outside. Picture frames, lamps, and various whatnots started falling to the floor. The harmonic sound of a trumpet caused the windows to shiver and the floor underneath them to tremble.

"What's happening?!" Chasity shouted as she fell to the floor.

When she looked around, Luke had vanished.

People going about their daily lives, unaware of what was coming, were stunned by the news that an unexplained phenomenon had erupted throughout the world.

For the Lord Himself will descend from heaven with a shout, with the voice of an archangel, and with the trumpet of God. And the dead in Christ will rise first. Then we who are alive and remain shall be caught up together with them in the clouds to meet the Lord in the air. And thus we shall always be with the Lord. (1 Thessalonians 4:16-17 NKJV)

CHAPTER 2

JANUARY 2021
(7 MONTHS EARLIER)

"Thank you, Natas, for the tour of the distribution facility," Mr. Denmart said with resounding approval, standing in the lobby of iTrack's undisclosed U.S. Headquarters. It was located thirty miles north of New Orleans, LA. "The tour was important for our sought-after government officials, politicians, celebrities, clergy members and local leaders who were still on the fence about getting the chip implanted. Now they can see what's waiting behind the scenes to be introduced to the world, and the impact it will have."

It was a typical winter Wednesday in January, with a morning temperature of 60 degrees. Jim Natas had sent his private jet to pick up key executives of Global Media Sources and individuals he believed would be key supporters of his implantable chip. He knew a tour of his underground distribution facility in southern Louisiana, and the sharing of the intimate details of its assembly, would ignite even more excitement and commitment.

"Absolutely," said Mr. Meyers. "Everyone was thoroughly impressed with your company and your team. And with the video presentation, House Representative Tadd Smith, Senator Nathaniel Johnson, Governor Luke Mann, Pastor Dobbs, and the others were able to see the front line manufacturing operation in Suzhou, China, and receive detailed explanations about the device. They all seemed comfortable with the answers to their questions. Now it's a matter of them sharing their comfort levels to recruit nationwide support of the chip."

"I can't praise digital technology enough," Mr. Denmart said.

"The sharing of information and the walk-through of the manufacturing operation were critical for them to see firsthand what we're asking them to support," Mr. Meyers said. "And the control it will provide to the Chosen System ruling all nations, and the targeted infrastructures fostering that control."

With an easy nod, Mr. Denmart said, "Many of them wanted to clear up any private doubts and get answers, prior to going public with their endorsement of the chip."

"Thank you for vetting our political movers and shakers. Their political records, high integrity, credibility, respect, and influence — as seen and supported by their constituents — is what we need to reach the masses," Natas said.

"Top quality, for sure. The work they're doing in their communities, and on a national level, places them high on the credibility list. But I can't take all the credit. Sam and our security team, and their relationship with law enforcement agencies throughout the world, are to be commended."

Mr. Denmart was momentarily distracted by several people in the conference center who were moving around, attending to the video and playback equipment.

He continued, "The gathering of information that helped facilitate our understanding of the people we targeted, including their lifestyle, financial security, and cautiously disciplined approach for making informed decisions about laws and policies to enact, has helped tremendously. This provided an understanding that included our financial, intelligence, and telecom partners, in particular. The ability to obtain data about their activities and the telephone transactions of whom they called, when they called, and how long the conversations lasted really helped our process determine who we could convince and trust. Whereas legitimate reasons would have normally been needed to obtain such data, our silent insiders were able to supply us with what we needed to make informed decisions about whom to pursue."

"I know it's been an exhausting process for your staff."

"Yes, it has. But we all know it was necessary."

"We know our chosen few will be perfect extensions of the ultimate prize. But being sworn to secrecy behind closed doors is more important," Natas said.

"Absolutely. With this group and those with whom we'll share tomorrow, we're free to focus on what matters most, and that's to build our New World Access movement," Mr. Denmart said.

"I hope everyone understood the reason for the secrecy of the distribution facility," Natas said bluntly. "I don't think House Representative Smith was too excited about being blindfolded."

As a young boy, Jim Natas, of British heritage, was exposed to tracking technology through the use of a microchip. Under the influence of his father, who was a scientist, Natas understood early on that the technology used for tracking airplanes through the use of Global Positioning Systems satellites could be shared with common people. This was an upgrade in technology that included an implantable chip to revolutionize the way the world would access and transact personal and business activities. Even more so, he knew the development of such a device would give its creator complete control over all beings. His creation would provide total access to personal identity information and geographic location through encoded bits of information embedded under a person's skin.

"I wouldn't think twice about it," Mr. Denmart said. "It was necessary. Just because we're trying to garner support, doesn't mean we can totally trust who we're trying to get that support from."

For years, Natas had worked with key governmental officials and foreign leaders throughout the world to get his implantable chip approved. His initial sales pitch was focused on connecting its use with that of the medical industry. The chip, inserted by certified medical personnel, would be able to access medical information in the event of an emergency. Emergency medical personnel would have immediate access to information that revealed which drugs a victim was allergic to. Upon arrival at the medical facility, the device would tell medical personnel the victim's complete medical history. What Natas was seeking now was the support of an elite group to foster a movement to make the implanting of his chip mandatory.

"With the teams we've assembled to increase public awareness, from merely chips in lost animals to the elimination of bank cards, credit cards, and membership cards, our mission is on track. Considering the array of personal information that will be inside one's body, making every one of their life transactions convenient, cost-effective, and safe, we are poised to have a lot of control and make a lot of money," Natas confirmed.

"Your collaboration with India's top technology gurus has really paid off," Mr. Denmart said with a slight smile.

"Just think—five years ago we were tossing around names for the device, from *My Access Chip* to *My True Access Chip*," Mr. Meyers said.

Natas interjected excitedly, "When you throw a 'dot com' at the end, I'm glad everyone agreed with my recommendation to keep it simple with *My Access Chip dot com*."

"Absolutely," Mr. Denmart said. "Myaccesschip.com. The world's modern day savior."

Praising the conclusion of a productive meeting, the three men walked to the entrance of the building and chatted while waiting for the transportation that would take Mr. Meyers and Mr. Denmart to the location of Natas' private jet.

Around 6'2" and 190 lbs., Natas was a handsome forty-year-old man, with pearl-like brown eyes, thick, curly eyebrows, and short, waxy brown hair. He always sported a freshly trimmed goatee. He was married with three kids, ages two, four, and ten. He was most admired for his charismatic, royal demeanor and affluent style of dress that routinely included a signature, lamb's wool, cashmere, sweater vest. He was a man of incredible distinction and presence.

Mr. Denmart, a petite man in his late fifties from York, PA, was often teased, due to his large, glassy, hazel eyes and Pinocchio nose. Divorced four times, he was feared because of his arrogance and God-like mentality. Currently living in New York, he had devoted his life to Global Media Sources. Before his reign ended, he wanted his legacy to be centered on how he used his clout to introduce and promote a life-transforming device that changed the world.

Matt Meyers, approaching his sixtieth birthday, was born in Richmond, VA, and grew up as a military brat. With his bald, shaved head, he was a tall, broad-chested man, a known bully who loved to drain the energy out of his subordinates. He was most proud of his fear-driven tactics.

"The name reinforces our message that people will be able to access any product or service with their implanted chip. For organizations and businesses currently using the system, it has meant a seamless offering of products and services, and the elimination of their customers circumventing their system, as well as theft and fraud," Natas said eagerly.

"And the way it's synced up with TV networks and syndicated radio stations, as well as My TrueAccess TV, My TrueAccess Radio, and the social networking tool iAccessagram, our in-your-face strategies are paying off," Mr. Meyers confirmed.

Standing expressionless, Mr. Denmart said, "I'm so pleased about all we've accomplished thus far to facilitate this movement."

"And gentlemen, once the world realizes the technology has been among us for decades, it'll be even more widely accepted. Everyone will be excited about the benefits of getting their access chip," Natas said.

"We'll need to continue to make sure our promotional tactics dispel any of the negative exploits about health hazards, misuse, and abuse," said Mr. Denmart.

"Especially those ministers like Pastor Stewart McFarland, who's been a thorn in our sides with his Antichrist and Mark of the Beast shenanigans," Mr. Meyers commented.

"Don't worry. Our teams are prepared," Mr. Denmart said with confidence. "Our haters, like Pastor McFarland and Senator Ryan Paul Patrick, continue to be on our radar."

"I know Pastor Conrad Dobbs has already been instrumental in the movement," Natas confirmed.

"I'm glad he was a part of the tour this morning," Mr. Denmart said.

"I'm sure that one million dollar donation to his church's building fund has helped," Natas said with a wide smile.

"And the one million to an offshore account for his personal pleasures," Mr. Meyers said with a pointed glance at Natas. "Our new round of promotional pitches will be packed with messages of convenience, cost-savings, and safety for consumers and businesses. Plus, a brief history lesson on the institution of the Social Security Number and comparable resistance will fuel our cause."

"And for those who need further convincing after all is released, we have people in place and events ready to create an even more heightened sense of urgency," Natas assured. "Right, Mr. Meyers?"

"Right. Larry Shepherd has recruited a new team of individuals who are poised to die for the movement," Mr. Meyers assured. "We're ready to pull the trigger on events that will motivate the masses to get the chip. And our politicians and leaders will be in place to console victims and grieving families by encouraging them to get chipped."

"And those natural disasters, such as earthquakes, hurricanes, tornadoes, tsunamis, typhoons, winter storms, and spring floods, will benefit us as well," Mr. Denmart commented.

"Yes, they are the sort of events we need…those that end in tragedy, like the typhoons in the Philippines, China, and Japan last year. Those sort of events are needed assets for us. Our team is working on a pitch as we speak that will present the *My Access Chip* as a key resource for identifying persons who are presumed dead," Mr. Meyers shared.

"Sad and unfortunate, but helpful to us," Natas said. "The goal is to create anxiety, concern, and ultimately panic. Our path to chip victory."

They all shared a grandiose laugh.

"Seriously, gentlemen, our news reporters are covering the grocery store break-ins and cash machine dismantling. I'm sure the looters see their actions as necessary, but with the chip, law enforcement personnel would be able to identify and capture these individuals. Our tracking devices would alert the police authorities and pinpoint the locations of these criminals, whether they're hiding on a boat or under a rock," Mr. Denmart stated.

"We're ready for the meeting tomorrow. The elite of the elite will be present, and after your presentation, I know they'll be ready to support the movement," Mr. Meyers said. "And thank you again for sending your jet to pick up everyone."

"Anything for the movement," Natas responded. "Have a safe trip back to Dallas. And I'll see you tomorrow morning."

An armored, bulletproof limousine pulled up in front of the undisclosed location. Men in black suits exited and ushered the gentlemen into the limousine, then Natas watched as they drove away down the dirt road.

The next day, in downtown Dallas, Texas, it was cold, windy, and dreary. Luke was in his cubicle, working on stats for his boss, Larry Shepherd. He noticed a large envelope with no return address, addressed to Mr. Shepherd, lying on the edge of his desk. The postal stamp indicated the origin as Beeville, Texas.

Who in the world would be sending Mr. Shepherd mail from Beeville, Texas? Luke thought to himself.

He picked up the envelope and walked down the hallways of Global Media Sources. All the employees knew it was an important day because Jim Natas and Mr. Denmart were scheduled to be in the building for a major meeting.

Luke stood in the doorway of Larry Shepherd's office. Larry was both worried and excited about the meeting. He was hoping for a huge promotion if the new group of executives and key supporters endorsed Mr. Natas' implantable tracking device. He'd been working on video and broadcast campaigns for weeks.

"Hi, Mr. Shepherd. An envelope was left on my desk for you," Luke said as he cheerily entered the office and handed Shepherd the envelope.

"Thanks," Larry replied abruptly.

Larry was sitting behind his desk, looking at a music video. He looked up at Luke and nodded for him to place the envelope on a table near his office door.

Recognizing the familiar sound and lyrics, Luke asked, "Is that an old video of that rapper duo Bone Esquire and Mo Money Monte?"

"Yes."

"Those two haven't performed together in a while."

"Yeah," Larry responded, sounding irritated.

"Are they getting back together?"

Larry nodded inattentively as he fast-forwarded through the video. "Mo Money Monte is in jail," he said coldly.

"Yes, I know. But my little brother, a fan of his music, says he's getting out soon. He keeps up with that sort of entertainment news."

"I'm sure you need to complete those stats for me," Larry said, looking intensely at Luke.

"Yes, sir, I do," Luke said, sounding amused. "I just thought this envelope from Beeville, Texas, might be important."

"Just sit it on my table."

"Who in the world would be sending you mail from Beeville, Texas?" Luke inquired. "I looked up the city, and the only major thing there is a prison."

Larry looked intensely at Luke. He was becoming noticeably agitated with Luke's questioning.

"Um…is that where Mo Money Monte is?" Luke asked.

Ignoring Luke completely, Larry continued looking at the video.

"It's going around the building that a major meeting is taking place today. Some important people from all over the world are going to be here." Luke said as he stood staring at Larry, waiting for a response.

"Yes, in about fifteen minutes. And if everything goes as I plan, I am going to be a rich man," Larry replied, then moved his chair back and stood up. He started to walk towards his office door, where Luke was standing.

"Wow. Don't forget the little people when you make it big."

"By the way, have you gotten your chip yet?"

Luke placed the envelope on the table and said, "No, sir!", then abruptly exited his office and hurried down the hallway.

All people entering the room were required to be patted and searched. They were also required to check in their cellular telephones and any devices with picture taking capabilities. Several Global Media Sources' personnel were standing around talking in the company's auditorium, waiting for the meeting to start. Samuel Cho and other Global Media Sources executives (from print, television, cable, radio, public relations, web marketing, and word-of-mouth marketing) stood near the entrance. They watched executives from Fortune 500 companies and leaders from various state and federal organizations, including ambassadors and dignitaries from various countries, file into the room.

Global Media Sources President Matt Meyers walked up behind Samuel Cho and tapped him on the shoulder, then gestured for Cho to follow him.

"Mr. Natas, I've been waiting to introduce you to Samuel Cho," Mr. Meyers said as he and Cho approached him and Mr. Denmart.

Mr. Meyers patted Cho on the back and began to share accolades about his work and background.

From a back door entrance, Larry Shepherd walked into the room. He quickly noticed Cho with Mr. Meyers, Mr. Denmart, and Jim Natas. He knew from their body movements that Cho was the topic of discussion. He walked quickly and stood next to Mr. Meyers, pretending to be interested in the ravings going on about Cho's value to the company.

"It's good to meet you, Cho. Mr. Meyers has said such wonderful things about you," Natas said. "He's told me about how great you are at executing pre-production, production, and post-production film projects. Commercials, cable TV programming, and infomercials."

"We're happy he's a part of our team now," Mr. Denmart said. "He owned a film production business for over twenty years before coming to us. We contracted a lot of work out to him before he became a part of the Global family."

"And he's exactly what we need for this next project," Mr. Meyers said.

Cho stood detached, looking at Mr. Natas and Mr. Denmart. Finally, he slowly responded, "Thank you." It was his first day back from a leave of absence to take care of his daughter.

"Yes, we have big plans for Cho!" Mr. Meyers said with excitement. "We just need to catch him up on everything that's been in the works over the passing months."

Looking at the entrance and those seated around the room, Larry interrupted Mr. Meyers and said, "I think everyone you're expecting has arrived, sir."

"Thank you, Larry. It's time we get started with the meeting. Natas, I know you're a busy man, so let's get this show on the road," Mr. Meyers said, walking off.

Mr. Meyers motioned for Natas and Denmart to sit near the head of the conference table. He looked at Cho and gestured for him to sit next to Natas. Larry observed the interactions and rushed to sit on the other side of Natas.

"Good morning, everyone!" Mr. Meyers said as he looked out into the audience.

There were mysterious looking men dressed in black suits starting to position themselves along the entrance doors and stage area. Photographers within Global Media Sources began to take pictures of Natas and those seated at the head table. To prevent the leaking of information not ready for public sharing, the photographers had been instructed to turn over the company-issued cameras after the meeting.

"I just want to thank everyone assembled here today for joining and supporting us in what will be the biggest launch of a product the world has ever known. We're particularly thrilled to have the maker of the product here. He's anxious to speak to you and share a presentation about his world-changing device."

Individuals in the audience began to applaud.

"First, let me say this room is filled with the global elite, who hold more worldwide power than ever forecast by our ancestors. Our combined power and status create a force that cannot be dismantled. Our abilities to understand, predict, and accelerate change are beyond the average person's comprehension. With a newfound, realistic approach to solve religious, social, economic, and political problems comes the revolutionary power of a tiny device that's stolen the hearts of many of us."

Applause and cheers began to resonate throughout the room.

Mr. Meyers began to raise his voice as the applause and cheers escalated. He continued by saying, "In our own private entities, we know having a person with a vision and broad capacity for leadership is paramount. His or her ability to influence and build teams and partnerships, under his/her control, typically works in the best interests of the organization. Well, just think about that same format for all nations combined; the idea of having one person with that vision and capacity to exert a deeper and more meaningful use of technology, guided by a timeless, abiding wisdom. Just thought I'd throw that concept out there as I introduced the man of the hour, Jim Natas. It's my opinion, and the opinion of many others, that he is that man. He's demonstrated ambition and passion for a better way of life for this world. That was the motivation behind his creation, or shall I say, his enhancement of technology."

Jim Natas stood and waved to the crowd.

Mr. Meyers continued, "His energy has the power to appeal to all social classes, ethnicities, generations, and genders."

Everyone in the audience stood and applauded vigorously, except for one person.

Mr. Meyers spoke loudly to bring the applause to a halt. He motioned for everyone to have a seat and said, "It's with great pleasure that I introduce to you Jim Natas of iTrack, Inc., from New Orleans, Louisiana."

The people in the audience stood again and began to applaud. Again, Mr. Meyers waited for the individuals to sit down and the applause to stop.

"Mr. Natas has been visionary in the evolution of an implantable chip that will revolutionize the world. I'm so excited that many of you from outside of the Global Media family were able to come today and get any questions you may have answered about the implantable chip."

Mr. Meyers began to acknowledge federal officials in attendance, like Tate Montgomery, who had been recently named to the Department of Homeland Security by the current administration, news anchors Jenny Purdue and Martin Maxwell, who would be covering breaking news reports, and Pastor Conrad Dobbs, who had brought members from his coalition of pastors.

"Based on the briefing documents everyone has seen, Natas is going to talk to us about a strategy for communicating important information about the new implantable device that's now being backed by our federal government. For those of you present today, we're grateful for the new 2021 administration and those of you who've worked diligently to revamp your products and program services to accommodate the acceptance of the chip.

And I'm especially grateful to those in our administration who have played a part in the enactment of *The Pledge*. Your support and work have been remarkable. You've helped us implement a clear strategy to garner the support of other major companies, medical facilities, and distributors. The chip revolution is well on its way because of you."

A parade of handclapping echoed throughout the room.

"But there are more initiatives and a lot more work that needs your attention. Now without further ado, I present to you the visionary of this hour, Jim Natas of iTrack, Inc."

Natas walked up the stairs to the stage with an unruffled movement, confidently approaching the podium. Mr. Meyers extended his hand to shake Natas' hand. The people in the audience began to stand, again, and applaud, again. Natas waited for the applause to stop, then began his remarks.

"It is indeed a pleasure to be here today. First, I want to thank Mr. Denmart, chairman and CEO of Global Media Sources, all the way from Manhattan, New York, and Mr. Meyers for their support of what has become known as a world changing device that my company has refined for everyday human use," Natas said, taking a deep breath. He switched from speaking English and greeted many of the dignitaries and diplomats from other countries in their native languages; Spanish, French, Arabic, Portuguese, Greek, Japanese, Vietnamese, Russian and over three dozen others.

He reached inside his suit jacket, pulled out a tiny object about one-third the size of a corn kernel, and held it up for everyone to see.

"It is so small that many of you probably can't even see it," Natas said, smiling. "I know many of you have heard and continue to hear a lot of rumors. Many of the rumors will include a lot of personal thoughts and feelings, and negative comments about this little object that has been tagged to have so much power for all of the wrong reasons. And, you will probably hear a number of scripture quotes. I know them all.

"*He causes all, both small and great, rich and poor, free and slave, to receive a mark on their right hand or on their foreheads, and that no one may buy or sell except one who has the mark or the name of the beast, or the number of his name.*" (Revelation 13:16-17 NKJV).

Natas quickly zoomed in on a man in the audience who was taking a notepad out of his coat jacket.

"I'm sure everyone was instructed upfront that there would not be any video recordings, pictures, or note taking, other than those of Global Media Sources' videographers and photographers," Natas said sternly.

One of the men dressed in black approached the man and whispered in his ear. The man promptly placed the notepad inside his jacket.

Natas continued, "First, let me assure you that this object has nothing to do with religion. It is a small tracking device that bears three sets of six numbers. When implanted into the right hand of a person, it's going to revolutionize our ability to identify, track, record, and monitor the comings and goings of every being on Earth. It's all about easy access and safety. For those of you here today that provide leadership over many products and services, this resource will be vital to your organizations. And as Mr. Meyers stated earlier, I want to thank those of you who have already revamped your infrastructure to accommodate the chip."

Cho's face became strained.

"We've worked with the top scientists, doctors, and researchers to master this product," Natas emphasized. "I know some of the materials you received before this presentation provide a list of basic features and benefits, but today I'll include its extended benefits. Benefits we're not quite ready for you to share with the public."

Mr. Meyers motioned for his secretary to turn on the projector. She did, then handed Natas a remote.

"During this presentation, I want to revisit and reemphasize the importance of this device." He held up the object. "This object provides opportunities far beyond the technology of cellular telephones and a variety of vehicular tracking devices. It will be extended, but not limited to, the buying and purchasing of food, clothing, housing, electronics—anything you can imagine consuming," Natas said.

Natas showed a video of a consumer in a grocery store selecting items and placing them in her specially designed grocery basket. When the consumer completed her shopping, rather than stand in a checkout line, the lady's items were captured as she entered a section to exit the grocery store, which used a sophisticated thermal imaging system paired with her implantable chip to scan and tally her costs. As she walked through the exit doors of the store, an automated voice said, "Thank you, Sally Mires, for shopping with us today. The total cost of $53.24 will be deducted from your Bank of Union checking account. You saved two dollars and thirty cents."

The audience was in awe of what the video had depicted. A few of the individuals in the audience were familiar with the technology, which was being piloted in select parts of the world.

"We already have this part of our project being piloted in select private grocery stores in a couple foreign countries and private communities in Canada and the United States," Natas described.

Cho sat thinking about a perceived invasion of privacy, major health side effects, and the fact that most people view such tools as a targeted tracking device for the government to spy on people.

"I know some of your followers will have concerns about privacy, as well as medical side effects, as we've seen with continued references to government spying. That's where all of you come into play, along with Global Media Sources' multilevel marketing campaign. That's by helping us diminish those negative perspectives," Natas responded, "and nurturing a targeted focus on the benefits, like these shown in my presentation."

Natas began to discuss the benefits recognized by a pet owner. "With a chip, a lost animal can be recovered and returned to its owner. Many of you who are pet owners know that's nothing new."

Various individuals in the audience turned and looked at one another, nodding in agreement.

Natas continued, "As approved by the U.S. Food and Drug Administration in 2004, this comparable type of microchip can be implanted in humans. For now, the information inside the chip houses the patient's health records. This is particularly critical when a patient cannot talk about his or her medical information. And now we're working with researchers at one of the universities to perfect the development of the implantable chip for soldiers, so the military can monitor their vital health information while they're out in the field. It can also be used for identification purposes. Even human trafficking organizations are looking into ways for prostitutes, drug addicts, and homeless persons to get the implant for free. Because of the activities they're involved in, their life span is often shortened. Most often, police officials are unable to identify them, and many of them are runaways and may have family looking for them. Mr. Lawrence, with the U.S. Department of Prison Bureaus, and other penal agencies are doing their part to help us by endorsing the product for testing purposes on inmates."

Mr. Meyers looked around the room, smiling.

"As you can tell from the various activities currently in place or underway, our expansion of the chip's capabilities will provide people with a more convenient way of life."

"Do you have the implantable chip?" Cho blurted out sarcastically.

Natas raised his right hand and said, "I most certainty do."

He held up a prototype of the device, again, for everyone to see, then said, "This microchip was inserted into the top of my hand with a syringe. A less than 5-minute procedure. No stitches. I've had it for five years and haven't incurred any health problems. My wife also has it, and my two, four, and ten-year-old kids have theirs."

Everyone in the room looked intensely at Natas' hand.

"I have access to my cars, computers, and my home with a simple wave of my hand."

Mr. Meyers stood up and said, "And it is our goal that everyone here today will get chipped."

Cho became agitated as he looked around the room, observing the excitement about Natas' chip. He became increasingly perplexed, and even more agitated. He looked up at Natas. He thought about his name. Thinking out loud in his head, he realized that if he rearranged the letters in Natas' name, it would display the word 'Satan'. His hands began to shake.

"For those of you ready to get chipped today, we have Dr. Simon here who is stationed in a private room down the hall," Mr. Meyers said loudly from his seat.

"Our goal is to introduce people all over the world to a comprehensive integrated worldwide system that provides a one-stop-shop movement to eliminate their credit cards, debit cards, rewards cards, discount store membership cards, driver's license I.D., Social Security cards, food stamp cards, gym membership cards, car and medical insurance cards, passport ID, key rings, passwords, and so much more. Also, tracking for those unfortunate instances related to natural disasters, terrorist attacks, bombings, company explosions, school shootings, rapists and child molesters. And for organizations like federal agencies, the U.S. Department of Health and Human Services, and local governmental agencies that offer services from health services, food stamps, WIC, to the Gold card, it'll provide the elimination of fraud—your users selling the products they're receiving for their personal monetary gain. For those on some sort of housing program, where the occupants have been authorized—well, we all know that in a lot of cases unauthorized relatives and friends are living in the dwelling with the authorized recipient. Requiring the authorized persons to be chipped will eliminate those sorts of fraudulent matters," Natas explained. "Special features of the chip will let us know who's in the house with the recipient at all times."

Everyone was amazed by Natas' presentation.

"Now, I know many of you were excited about the smart chip credit card that surfaced a few years ago, and the global ease and security it provided for making transactions. People didn't think twice about receiving a new credit card that had a visible chip. For employers who transitioned to employee ID cards with an embedded chip for keyless entry, employees didn't think twice about waving their ID card in front of a reader to access their building. For those of you who are parents, when the school district informed you about its transition to a school ID card with a chip inside to monitor the movements of students, you didn't think twice. I assure you, *The My Access Chip* transcends the smart chip credit card's capability and far exceeds any other comparable technology."

Used and supported by the United States, Europe, Canada, Mexico, Asia, and South America, the smart chip credit card was equipped with a chip encrypted with the consumer's card information, protecting it from fraud. Now that comparable technology could be inside the person and contain infinite information.

"Global Media Sources' media outlets, like their cable news, entertainment, print, and radio stations, will be instrumental in developing campaigns that promote and encourage the chip," Natas said proudly. "Many of you here in the room today widely support the chip and know it will ultimately become a mandatory way of life in the very near future. Mexico law enforcement agencies are already piloting the chip for the purposes of monitoring criminal activity."

As the audience applauded in excitement, Natas smiled. Automatically, he gave a nod of his head, accepting the applause. He tried repeatedly to continue his talk, but the applause of support continued. Knowing he wasn't finished yet, he began to show a mixture of awkwardness and emotion.

He continued to speak through the loud applause and said, "The power of the implantable chip is so great! Beyond what many of you have started to comprehend. Many of you have heard the reference to *New World Access*. The implantable chip is the platform for a superior system that will enable control of a global unified government, monetary system, and religion. It's time to end global division. With nearly eight billion people that make up the world population, we have a long way to go. Right now, it's estimated that four billion have been chipped, but we're no way close to the actual world population of 7.8 billion. Our goal is to have the remaining three-point-something billion chipped by August this year. That's an aggressive goal of hitting the pavement hard and heavy. But, with all of you helping to promote our *MyAccessChip* using your community and business platforms along with social media, we'll meet that number."

The audience began to applaud relentlessly, and Natas appeared to get emotional, again.

Cho shifted in his chair, becoming increasingly uneasy with what Natas was saying to the audience. He glanced over at Mr. Meyers and Mr. Denmart, trying to control his disapproval.

They act like this man is the next Pope or something, Cho thought to himself. *He demonstrates to them how his system can record health information, eliminate the use of cards, and keep every family safe by using numbers to track members. If the system is for people to track their family members, then apparently the maker of this product can track anyone. Then he casually mentioned the New World Access. Why can't they see it's all about tracking and controlling us? It really is about biblical prophecy in the works.*

He causes all, both small and great, rich and poor, free and slave, to receive a mark on their right hand or on their foreheads, and that no one may buy or sell except one who has the mark or the name of the beast, or the number of his name. (Revelation 13:16-17 NKJV).

Mr. Denmart stood up and said, "All of us here today have a responsibility to not only endorse this product, but to help Global Media Sources reinforce why it's going to be vital to our everyday existence."

With a straightforward, inescapable voice of power, Natas said, "And when reinforcing its necessary existence, always remember that accidents and disasters such as plane and train crashes, earthquakes, tornadoes and tsunamis, and bombings are our friends. As well as those attacks by homegrown and international terrorists. They all will help you as messengers, and our Global Media Sources news teams emphasize over and over why everyone must get the chip."

"Suppose the people reject the chip? What are the alternatives?" Cho said aloud, boldly.

Natas appeared lost in thought for a moment, as if to choose his next words carefully, then said, "I'm afraid there are no alternatives. For those who choose not to get chipped, once it's mandatory, they will suffer dire consequences."

The people in the audience began to look around at one another.

The insinuations of Natas' statement left Cho wordless, his dedicated mind staggering.

"For those of you wondering if such power exists, just know it does," Natas said. "Moving forward, you'll start hearing more about the Pledge campaign."

"Over the next six months, there will be strategic demonstrations that will dramatize the seriousness of accepting the My Access Chip," Mr. Denmart said assuredly. "Planned activities that will impact the entire world."

Cho sat, remaining silent. He wondered exactly what Mr. Denmart meant by saying planned activities that would impact the entire world. As he further analyzed Natas' words in his head, Natas continued to speak about his company's device and its revolutionary implications. Cho began to reflect on the teachings he'd received regarding the False Prophet, Antichrist, and the Mark of the Beast.

In his office, at his desk, Cho started to doodle. He stared repeatedly at the piece of paper he'd written on.

"Looks like you were apprehensive about iTrack at the meeting today," Larry said, walking into Cho's office.

"Do you want something in particular?" Cho said as he got up from his seat, walked towards his door, and placed his left hand on the knob.

"Yeah. I want to know why everyone makes such a fuss over you," Larry said with sarcasm as he walked out. "That will all change over the next six months."

CHAPTER 3

On his drive home, Larry began to reminisce about his humble beginnings and his goal of someday becoming the executive producer of Global Media Sources' broadcasting system. Willing to trample anyone necessary to achieve his goal, Larry intended to use his twenty years with Global Media Sources, his education, his community influence, his family, and his position as deacon in the church to advance his personal agenda.

"How was work today, honey?" Larry's wife, Betty, asked as he entered the kitchen.

She stood at the stove in their kitchen, stirring and adding butter to a pot of mashed potatoes. Rain was hitting the windows. She placed a sample on the spoon and extended it for Larry to taste it. Ignoring Betty, he looked at the place settings on their dining room table.

He placed a folder on their granite counter top and said, "Mashed potatoes, again. What else did you cook?"

"Baked fish with grilled squash and zucchini."

"Why can't you ever cook some real meat?" Larry asked in an angry tone. "Some steak, fried pork chops, fried catfish? You need to get some tips from my mother. Somebody who knows what I like to eat. You'd think after nearly thirty years, you'd know."

Betty tried not to react to Larry's comments. She'd almost become immune to his verbal insults.

"'Cause that's not how Jesus ate," Betty's mother yelled out. "Read your Bible. It says, *They gave him a piece of broiled fish.*" (Luke 24:42 NKJV)

Betty's mother, Claudia McIntyre, had recently come to live with them. The progression of Alzheimer's had resulted in Betty having to take over her mother's daily care, as well as her financial and legal affairs.

"Why is your mother here again?" Larry said cruelly, looking at Mother McIntyre, who was sitting in her special chair. He sat down at the bar and started to read the contents of the folder.

"Hi, William," Mother McIntyre said pleasantly to him. "I wondered what took you so long to come and see your sister."

Shaking his head, Larry looked at Betty and said, "There she goes again, thinking I'm her brother."

"You've gained some weight," Mother McIntyre said. "You'd better go on a diet so you can get a girlfriend."

"This is crazy! Why did I ever agree to let her come live with us?" Larry said, steadily shaking his head at Mother McIntyre. "I need to go make a telephone call."

He got up from the counter and started walking towards his study.

"I'm still praying for you to get a girlfriend, lose weight, and get married, William."

Larry looked back at his mother in-law with contempt.

"Wait, Larry! Is everything okay? You seem somewhat agitated," Betty said.

Larry turned and looked intently at Betty, then walked back into the kitchen and stood in front of her and said, "Earlier today, my company publicly announced its partnership with iTrack, the manufacturer of the revolutionary implantable chip. Today, I was chipped. And now, it'll be necessary that you, the kids, and your mother get chipped."

"No, Larry! No!" Betty exclaimed. "I've been listening to Pastor McFarland on satellite radio. He's the pastor at Triumphant Baptist Church who's warning people about what's coming. He's doing a series about the signs of end times. In his series, he's talking about false prophets and the events they'll use to cause people to faint with fear. The other day, he talked about the time when Jesus will appear in the sky, the trumpet will sound, and angels will gather God's elect. I know I wanna be one of God's elect."

Larry stared at Betty with rage growing in his eyes.

Betty continued and said, "I'm not doing what Pastor McFarland is preaching against on the radio. He's warning us and telling us to read our Bibles. See, I've written down this scripture from his message yesterday."

Larry hesitated for a moment, then took his right hand and slapped Betty in her face. The blow was so hard, she fell to the floor.

Emotionally out-of-control, Larry said, "This is what the mighty chipped hand does to someone who's disobedient."

"You are CRAZY! That company has you CRAZY!" Betty shouted. Bracing herself on the corner of the countertop, she stood up, reached for her notepad, and held it up. "Look," she shouted.

Written on the notepad was:

If anyone worships the beast and his image, and receives his mark on his forehead or on his hand, he himself shall also drink of the wine of the wrath of God, which is poured out full strength into the cup of His indignation. He shall be tormented with fire and brimstone in the presence of the holy angels and in the presence of the Lamb. And the smoke of their torment ascends forever and ever; and they have no rest day or night, who worship the beast and his image, and whoever receives the mark of his name. (Revelation 14:9-11 NKJV)

Mother McIntyre yelled out in distress, "Don't hit your sister!" She reached for the telephone. "I'm calling the police. Someone has to stop you from hitting your sister."

Larry walked quickly over to Mother McIntyre and knocked the telephone from her reach.

Hysterical, Betty shouted, "Larry, please don't hit my mother."

As he walked over to Betty, she raised her arms in a half-hearted attempt to protect herself from the progressive onslaught of Larry's rage and placed her head in her hands.

Larry was silent for a few moments, then said, "First of all, Pastor Dobbs is our pastor. That's who you should be listening to. Not some non-progressive, small-minded preacher. I don't ever want to hear you mention McFarland in this house again."

"Why are you yelling at your sister, William? Are you okay? You seem irritated," Mother McIntyre asked.

"Everything's okay, Mother," Betty said.

"William sure has gotten mean. Must be the weight gain."

Betty lifted her head out of her hands. Shaking and shivering with fear, she said, "Pastor Dobbs wants you to call him about the Men's Conference next month. He says it's urgent."

"Why didn't you tell me that first thing?" Larry snapped.

Betty had spent almost thirty years in a controlling, loveless marriage riddled with verbal abuse. Larry had never hit her, but she knew the day would come and it had. She was willing to endure Larry's treatment towards her, though, for the sake of an image she'd created and wanted to maintain. From all appearances, they represented the perfect couple. Spiritually mature. Financially secure. Emotionally stable. Socially connected.

"I don't know who it is, but someone named Mo Money Monte called collect for you today. I didn't accept the charges."

"Good for you," Larry replied.

"Why would he be calling you collect?"

"Stop asking me a bunch of questions! I'll tell you what I want you to know."

As Mother McIntyre raised the volume on the TV, both Larry and Betty were distracted by a story that appeared on the news station. At that moment, Larry's cell phone rang. He started to walk down the hallway to his study.

"Are you leaving already, William?" Mother McIntyre asked. "I need some toothpaste for my teeth. Take that check I wrote out for you and get me some."

He whispered to the caller, "Looks like it's happened."

Turning back towards Betty, Larry hung up his cell phone and said, "I've gotta get back to the office."

"What about dinner?"

"More fish for you and your mom. I might not be home tonight. My team has to get on the coverage of some hotel bombings and plane crashes that just happened."

"Where?" Betty asked.

"That's why I've gotta get to the news station!"

Larry hurried out the door. After he'd left, Betty moved closer to the TV to listen to the news anchor.

"We're receiving reports of simultaneous hotel bombings in Washington, D.C., Sioux Falls, South Dakota, Sante Fe, New Mexico, and London. The list is growing. Now coming in are plane crashes in New York City, Seattle, Washington, and Bismarck, North Dakota. The list is growing," the news anchor reported.

"Where is your mean husband going?" Mother McIntyre yelled out. "Tell your pastor to read him the scripture from first Peter, chapter three, verse seven: likewise, husbands, live with your wives in an understanding way, showing honor to the woman as the weaker vessel, since they are heirs with you of the grace of life, so that your prayers may not be hindered. Maybe he'll treat you better."

"Larry Shepherd asked me about getting the chip earlier today," Luke said, sitting across from Chasity Meyers at Café Shade, their favorite sandwich shop.

"You need to do it. I've gotten mine. See." Chasity extended her hand. "You know I have to get it since I'm the boss' daughter. But I would have gotten it anyway. For me, it's no different than getting a body piercing or tattoo."

"Well, I wouldn't get a body piercing or tattoo or any markings on my body, and I certainly don't intend to get the chip," Luke said in a forceful tone.

"And why not? I have a couple of tattoos," Chasity said. "I can't show you where I had a piercing done, in the belly button and…" Chasity smiled and showed Luke the tattoo of her boyfriend's name, Bone Esquire, on her shoulder, and a rose on her ankle. "Stop being a nerd," she exclaimed.

"I'm not being a nerd, just standing firm about something I've decided not to do."

"Does the Bible say not to do it?" Chasity inquired.

"Read this scripture, Leviticus nineteen, verse twenty-eight - *Ye shall not make any cuttings in your flesh for the dead, nor print any marks upon you: I [am] the LORD.* It literally doesn't say don't do it; it says don't do it for the burial of the dead. In Middle Eastern cultures, it was believed that the spirit of the dead hung around for three days before being sent to the afterlife. According to my pastor, we see this even in Jewish beliefs. When Lazarus died, Jesus waited to come until the fourth day, and the sisters said, 'Lord, had You been here earlier, Lazarus could have lived.' In this belief, the families of the dead would cut themselves and carve family symbols into their bodies, believing it created a portal for the spirit of the deceased to enter them. We also see this in the Bible when Elijah and the prophets of Baal had their face-off. The Bible says that as the prophets of Baal became desperate, they began to cut themselves."

"Um…interesting," Chasity responded, laughing. "Too deep for me. All I know is you need to get chipped soon."

"Strangely enough, this cutting phenomenon has made a resurgence, especially in young women. This cutting, today, is a matter of self-loathing and hate; however, its roots are in creating an entrance for a spirit to possess you."

"Wow! Well, enough about that if you're not getting a tattoo because of some mumbo jumbo. So, what are you eating? I can't be here too long. I need to meet Bone later on."

"I thought he went AWOL on you?" Luke inquired.

"He's going through some things, trying to produce his next album. He's had to do a lot on his own since Mo Money Monte's been locked up. Plus, he's getting ready to be a part of a big movement."

"I see."

"He even thinks I'm good enough to record on one of his tracks with him," Chasity said with tense excitement.

"I walked in on Mr. Shepherd listening to one of their old tracks."

"Yes, for the new video introducing the chip. I know he was editing and inserting new footage," Chasity informed him. "Hopefully, Mo Money Monte will be getting out soon, so they'll be able to get back on top. I can't wait to see my man doing his thing with his boy again. And hopefully, me alongside him. There's talk of a mega tour and a bunch of other stuff."

Luke, looking disturbed, said, "I thought you were going to Bible study with me this evening? My pastor is continuing his series on end time prophecy."

"I'm so sorry, I need to see Bone," Chasity said. "Maybe next week. Let's order, I'm hungry. You need to eat for all those marathons you be training for."

"Right."

"You're paying, right?" Chasity asked.

"Sure."

"Plus, Mr. Larry has invited me to his church for Bible study. My dad likes Pastor Dobbs and his teachings."

Luke was interested in more than a friendship with Chasity, but he knew she was still hung up on Bone Esquire. He believed Bone was just using Chasity because of her father's influence, but he realized she had to see it for herself.

At home with his wife, Malin, and daughter, Adrika, Cho thought about the content of the meeting and how he'd ended up at Global Media Sources. It was over two years ago the unexpected happened on a sunny July morning. Cho's business site, comprised of three adjoining buildings on an acre of land, was burned down. While working on a high priority contract for Global Media Sources, one of Cho's employees ran inside, yelling that the storage building was on fire and the fire was quickly spreading to the second building. Cho yelled out to his other employees to run outside. He didn't realize that his daughter was on the property until he saw her car parked on the side of one of the buildings. Once he realized his daughter might be inside, he ran towards the building. The fire trucks had just arrived. One of his employees held him back. Cho cried out for his daughter.

The firefighters immediately started hosing the building down with water. All three buildings were engulfed in flames. Once the firefighters were able to contain the flames, they entered the building where Cho believed his daughter was located. It was the building that housed equipment and machinery, as well as living quarters for those times when Cho needed to stay on the property. His daughter, an aspiring model, had retreated there after one of her photo shoots. One of the firefighters quickly exited with Cho's daughter in his arms. She was badly burned and barely breathing.

Cho had lost his business, the one thing he'd built from the ground up that allowed him to support his family. Now he worked for Global.

"How did Adrika's doctor's appointment go today?" Cho asked his wife, Malin, as he entered the living room.

Their daughter had been severely burned in the fire that destroyed Cho's business. She'd undergone numerous surgeries and was disfigured beyond recognition.

"Malin, did you hear me?" Cho said.

His wife was sitting on the sofa, sorting through a pile of medical bills.

"It went well, I guess. She'll need physiotherapy once a month now."

"That's better than every day."

"I know," Malin said. "She's thinking about shaving her head."

"What?" Cho shouted.

"She simply can't bear the way she's losing her hair."

"Absolutely not!" Cho exclaimed.

"It's not your decision. She was burned over 50% of her body. In a coma for ten weeks. In the hospital for nearly six months. Not only is she scarred emotionally and physically…"

Malin started to cry. Cho sat down beside her to console her.

"It'll be okay. Go and check on your daughter," Malin said.

As Cho stood up and proceeded to walk towards his daughter's bedroom, he received a call on his cell phone.

"Hello," Cho answered. Malin noticed his disturbed look as Cho listened to the caller. After the telephone call ended, Cho frantically said, "I've gotta go back into the office. Something terrible has happened."

"What?" Malin asked.

"There have been some hotel bombings and plane crashes."

"Where?"

"I just know one of the hotel bombings was at a hotel in D.C.," Cho said. "I've gotta get back to the office."

"What about Adrika?"

"I'll be back as soon as I can," Cho said as he ran out the door. "I'll call her. Love you, honey."

For four years, Mo Money Monte had been the ideal prisoner at the Beeville State Prison. Since his stay in prison, Mo Money Monte had given his life to Christ. He'd been working on various programs with the prison chaplain, Pastor Stewart McFarland, which included multiple Bible study classes during the week. As he looked forward to a future release date and continuing his Christian work once he got out, he was shanked by another prisoner. He was rushed to a nearby hospital, where he'd been under treatment for two weeks for life-threatening wounds.

"Good morning, sir," Mo Money Monte's doctor said as he walked into his hospital room. A nurse in her early thirties followed closely behind him, carrying a tray of medication.

"Good morning, Doctor," Mo Money Monte said, speaking softly.

"I'm Doctor Simon," the doctor said. "I'm taking over for Doctor Millsap. He's on vacation."

Mo Money Monte, an African American male in his late twenties, was sitting upright in his bed, wearing his prison-issued clothing.

"Nice to meet you, Doctor Simon. I think," Mo Money Monte said with a weak smile. "It's freezing in here."

"Yes, I know. It's always cold in here."

"Right!"

"You're doing remarkably well for someone who was stabbed twice in the chest, several times in the back, in your abdomen, and legs," Doctor Simon said while looking at Mo Money Monte's chart.

The nurse sat the tray on a table.

"I just thank God for doctors like you and Doctor Millsap," Mo Money Monte said gratefully. "As I told Nurse Hobbs, I was stabbed by a fellow inmate because of his hatred for me and the ministry work I've dedicated my life to while in prison."

The nurse, Pamela Hobbs, moved closer to his bed.

"That's unfortunate," Doctor Simon said. "I don't know if anyone's mentioned it to you, but we're inserting the implantable chip here at the hospital. In your case, it'll help your family members know what's happening to you while you're in prison. It's free for inmates. I just need you to sign some consent forms."

Mo Money Monte looked troubled as Doctor Simon continued talking about an implantable chip.

"Thank you, Doctor, but I'm not interested."

"Think about it. You can get it done during your stay here. I'll check on you later. Nurse Hobbs is going to check your vitals."

The doctor left the hospital room.

"How are you doing this morning, Nurse Hobbs?" Mo Money Monte said, still disturbed by the doctor's comment about the chip.

"I'm good."

"I can't believe he asked me about getting an implantable chip."

"Yes. They're encouraging all of us, as health professionals, to get chipped. Especially since our medical facilities are responsible for chipping people."

"Have you gotten chipped?" Mo Money Monte asked.

"No, my pastor has spoken out against it. He talks about it being a menace to society, that it'll serve as a deadly plague for all who get it."

"Who's your pastor?"

"Pastor Stewart McFarland. I attend Triumphant Baptist Church."

"Pastor Stewart McFarland? He's over our prison ministry."

"Small world."

"WOW!"

"Right now, the chip is voluntary. According to Pastor McFarland, he foresees a movement to make it mandatory. I'm thinking Doctor Millsap's absence may have something to do with his non-acceptance of the chip."

"Really?" Mo Money Monte responded.

"You should ask Pastor McFarland about the chip the next time you see him."

"So, are you going to get chipped?"

"No."

"What will you do if it really does become mandatory?"

"Die," Nurse Hobbs confidently replied. She quickly changed the subject and said, "By the way, did you call your father?"

"Yes," Mo Money Monte responded. "He wasn't at home. And the reality is, he's probably avoiding my attempts to communicate with him."

"I can try and get in touch with him for you. He needs to know what happened to you, again."

"It's pointless, Nurse Hobbs. I've been locked up for nearly four years, and my dad hasn't come to visit me once."

"Maybe he doesn't know you're in prison."

"He knows."

"Maybe he can help with an early release."

"Maybe if there was some value for him in doing so. Otherwise, I doubt it," Mo Money Monte said.

The one thing Mo Money Monte missed in his life was a relationship with his biological dad, Larry Shepherd. His mother, who was Caucasian, was a casual acquaintance of Larry's. When she told Larry she was pregnant, he promised to take care of her and her baby, but he told her his wife could never know about the child and that he wouldn't be a part of the child's life. Mo Money Monte's mother ended up marrying a man who was verbally and physically abusive to him and his siblings. Mo Money Monte found refuge in the gangsta lifestyle (drugs, alcohol, guns) the neighborhood he grew up in had to offer. Longing for a connection with his father, as an adult Mo Money Monte tried to connect with Larry on two occasions, but his father wouldn't have anything to do with him.

"I've only seen my father twice in my life. Once when my stepfather broke my collar bone after beating me."

"What happened?" Nurse Hobbs asked.

"It was just another one of those times when he would get drunk or high and beat me, my siblings, or my mom," Mo Money Monte said. "My mother called my biological father because she needed help with the medical bills. He actually came to the hospital and brought her some money with the instructions not to contact him again. And the second time was when I was getting ready to graduate from high school. I found out where he lived and followed him one day to an auto parts store."

"What happened?" Nurse Hobbs asked.

"I walked into the store. He saw me immediately and knew who I was. I look just like him. He asked me what I was doing there, and I said I wanted to talk to him. The bottom line is, he said for me to never make contact with him again."

"Wow!" Nurse Hobbs said in amazement. "I thought you said your dad was prominent in the community with various social programs and is a deacon in his church?"

"Yes, he is," Mo Money Monte responded. "And from what I've Googled about him, he's involved in a lot of community events associated with his church and sits on all sorts of boards and committees."

"I'm sure he'd be proud of you if he knew about the work you're doing with the prison ministry," Nurse Hobbs stated.

"All my dad cares about is that no one finds out about his illegitimate son," Mo Money Monte said.

"That's so sad. I don't understand secretive, deceitful men like that, who pretend to be good, righteous church men," Nurse Hobbs said.

"I'm just glad I know my biological father. Hopefully, one day I can help him become a true righteous man."

"I too know what it's like not to have your biological father in your life. My stepfather was a horrible man. My sister and I met our real father about five years ago. He's the greatest. There's nothing we wouldn't do for him."

While Nurse Hobbs was talking, Mo Money Monte looked up at the television. "Can you turn up the volume? It looks like something serious has happened."

She retrieved the remote and turned up the volume. A news reporter was giving an account of a bombing at a hotel in D.C.

The news reporter said, "It has been reported that two telephone calls were placed to the hotel's front desk, warning of an imminent bombing. Minutes later, a blast ripped through the D.C. historic hotel. It is estimated that several hundred guests have been killed or injured."

"We're running out of safe places," Nurse Hobbs said in a melancholy tone.

"Really sad."

"What about that song you've written?" Nurse Hobbs said to change the subject. "Can you share a little of it with me?"

"Only if you promise not to sell it," Mo Money Monte said, laughing.

"Definitely not!"

"Okay, here goes. I wrote it after my first stabbing and call it *Awakened to His Presence.*"

"Nice, I like that title."

"When I awoke and felt the pain of that shank that had penetrated my flesh, You revealed to me it was for my protection from my self-imposed mess. Denied by my daddy. Dismissed by my mother. Deserted by love. I sought a life infested with becoming a superstar so I could get the respect I thought I deserved. Thank You, Lord, for not giving up on me. You got my attention in Your own way, and now I'm in Your presence, convicted to serve You every day. In pursuit of a life filled with Your Holy Spirit and Peace, I'm glad my mind is no longer restricted to my self-fulfilling prophesy. Now it's funny when I think how I never acknowledged You, now I can't imagine my life without You. No longer a prisoner of TDCJ, but a servant of my Lord and Personal Savior, who uses me every day. Free to forgive. Absent of anger. Delivered from self-destruction. I'm so grateful You denied me death, so now I spend the rest of my life giving You my best."

After a few more days in the hospital, Mo Money Monte was returned to the prison.

Bone Esquire, a young white man in his mid-twenties from the affluent neighborhood of Highland Park, was born to a pedigree of Irish immigrants who made their fortune as whiskey makers. Accustomed to a lifestyle rooted in wealth and privilege, Bone preferred to hang around friends who shared his love for rap music.

Mo Money Monte was his best friend, who had shown him everything he needed to know about the rap game. His talent for helping Mo Money Monte write lyrics that expressed the politics, sex, and violence that resonated with oppressed communities won the two of them recognition throughout various countries. But their rocket-speed path to stardom was not without consequences. With their fame came the perils of envy and jealousy from many, and the pitfalls of a glorified lifestyle riddled with women and sex, cars, houses, jewelry, and drugs.

At the height of their music career, Mo Money Monte was stopped one night by the police. After a search of his vehicle, drug paraphernalia and a large amount of cocaine, heroin, and methamphetamines were found in the trunk of his car, along with $15,000 in cash and a Smith & Wesson 9mm.

In court, the sworn police officer that arrested him disputed Mo Money Monte's claim that the drugs, money, and gun had been planted by the officer. He testified that the drugs, money, and gun were in Mo Money Monte's possession. Mo Money's attorney was not able to convince the jury beyond a reasonable doubt that the officer planted the items. As a result, Mo Money Monte was convicted and sent to prison.

Bone Esquire was in the studio of his new label, Platineum Records, working on arrangements for his upcoming album. He and his audio engineer, Spider Man, were sitting at the audio console, waiting to meet with the vice president and producer of Platineum Records.

"I hear your boy is getting out of jail in a few days, or within the month," said Spider Man.

For months, there had been rumors of Mo Money Monte's release. Spider Man started to play around with some mixes he'd created for one of the tracks.

"Yeah. I know he's gonna like the lyrics to this new song," Bone replied. "I like that sound."

"Have you talked or visited with Mo?" Spider Man asked. He was curious about their level of contact, since Bone never mentioned Mo Money Monte.

"No, I haven't had time," Bone responded.

"I heard he's different now," Spider Man said.

"What are you talking about?"

"I heard he's all religious now."

"How do you know?"

"I have friends in the pen. So, I doubt he'll be interested in your lyrics," Spider Man said, "and that's gonna be a huge problem for you."

"If the religious change-over is really true, I know he'll come around once he understands what's at stake. Mo is all about the Benjamins," Bone assured him. "That part of him will never change."

"If you say so. Why don't you try a couple of your lyrics to the music?" Spider Man suggested.

Bone started to rap words from his new song, *Big Brother vs. the Preacher Man.*

"Big Brother. My guardian angel. Here to protect us from a world of danger. We can't see it right now. But a collapse is coming. Our only means of survival is the 'my access chip' inserted where they say I wanted it. You ask me how I know. Because of my main man, Mo. Don't be deceived. The preacher man claims it's a prophecy. But I'm here to tell you it's his attempt to sway you, so Big Brother can't save you. Oh, Preacher Man. Oh, Preacher Man. I know you don't want Big Brother to succeed. All because the chip will stifle your greed. Preacher Man, the 'my access chip' is not a sign of the end. It's just my guardian angel's protection seed."

Spider Man smiled and said, "That's tight, Bone. I can't wait for the video."

"The lyrics are also part of a campaign Larry Shepherd of Global Media Sources wanted me to write," Bone said. "There's some powerful stuff happening. A movement beyond comprehension. And all of us will be a catalyst for shaping it worldwide."

"So, is Mo Money Monte okay with everything? Especially you signing with Platineum Records?" Spider Man asked.

"I haven't told him yet," Bone responded.

"What?"

"I haven't told him," Bone said intensely. "He's in jail. He's in no position to make decisions about our future."

"That's wrong, man," Spider Man said with disappointment. "How you gonna sign with a new label without telling him?"

"He'll be okay. Once he finds out his daddy, Larry Shepherd, is involved, I promise you he'll be on board. He'll do anything to get close to his daddy."

"Um…visitation. Communication. People make decisions about their business, etc., in prison all the time."

"Don't say anything," Bone said softly. "Mole, the vice president of Platineum Records, will be here shortly."

"Now by that statement, I'm assuming he doesn't know Mo Money Monte doesn't know you've switched labels and included him in the switch?"

"No, he doesn't."

"And I'm assuming he saw Mo Money Monte's signature on some contract?" Spider Man said.

"Mo Money Monte has been locked up for four years. I'm the one on the outside trying to keep our team together. They never would have signed me alone."

"What team? Team members communicate. You haven't even been in contact with Mo Monday Monte!"

"Stop minor thinking."

"What in the world is 'minor thinking?'"

"Stop thinking minor. Mo Money Monte is gonna be pleased with the deal I agreed to for us," Bone said. "There are millions of dollars in the works for us. And like I said, he'll do anything for his daddy."

"I sure hope so. Word on the street is, he'll be getting out soon."

"The word on my street says his stay is gonna be extended. That is, until everything's in place," Bone said. "Don't ask me how I know."

"Okay…"

"Platineum Records is well-funded and organized. They have connections you wouldn't believe. Nothing like that little grass-roots, garage-size label, MasterMark," Bone said. "In this competitive market, you've got to go with the big dogs who can make you bigger than life."

"Yeah. Well, MasterMark is who got you all to the fame level you're experiencing. I don't think Mo Money Monte is gonna be pleased that you ditched his homeboys."

"It'll be good."

"The only producer he ever really trusted was Smiley," Spider Man said.

"Just be glad I got them to agree to accept you," Bone informed Spider Man.

"So, do you have this chip you're rapping about?" Spider Man asked.

"Yes, I do. And you'll need to get it as well," Bone said.

"I'm not sure I want some foreign object inside my body."

"I guarantee you—you won't know it's there. I have the latest of the greatest technology. Have you ever gotten a splinter in your finger?"

"Yes. And it hurts!"

"Well, what I have is small, like half the size of a corn kernel, and it doesn't hurt. Implanted inside my right hand is this chip that contains more information than you could ever imagine."

Spider Man stared intensely at Bone's right hand.

"And this is what we're gonna get millions of dollars for, to help Global Media Sources promote it to the masses," Bone shared.

"That's deep. If I'm a recipient of those millions, then I'm definitely onboard."

Mr. Mole walked into the studio while talking on his cellular phone. His facial expression was consumed with despair. Moments later, his telephone call ended.

"Hi, Mr. Mole," Bone said. "Is everything okay?"

"My producer, Geomack's, plane has crashed in New York's Hudson River," Mr. Mole said, a bit frantic.

"Are there any survivors?" Bone asked.

"No one can tell me," Mr. Mole responded.

"I can call my contact at Global Media and ask him," Bone said.

"Please. See what you can find out for me," Mr. Mole said. "Call me and let me know what you find out. Sorry guys, I can't meet with you now. My secretary will reschedule. Bone let me something asap."

CHAPTER 4

Global Media Sources had the best people in the world on the ground, covering accidents and disasters. They were particularly proud of Jenny Purdue and Martin Matthews, award-winning TV news anchors for their My TrueAccess News Flagship Program and My TrueAccess World News, along with Matt Nicholas from their My TrueAccess Radio Program. All were well known for covering critical stories such as the aftereffects of the September 11th terrorist attacks, Boston Marathon Bombing, and Toronto Train Derailment. Cho and Larry's teams were responsible for the preparation of news stories, along with the oversight and execution of key video and graphic elements.

"What's going on out there?" Mr. Meyers asked as he entered the control room.

There were a series of breaking news stories being prepared by the various teams. Mr. Meyers was most interested in the bombing that had occurred in Washington, D.C., and the American Airways Boeing 777 that crashed in New York's Hudson River. Information regarding the events was spilling in from remote locations.

Cho responded and said, "Our London news tourist lives in New York, and our China news tourist is in Washington, D.C. Both are covering the stories."

"Great! Keep me posted," Mr. Meyers said as he walked out.

Mr. Meyers saw Larry walking down the hall towards him with a cup of coffee.

"Project My Access Chip has started," Larry said with enthusiasm as he stopped.

"Now. Those campaigns and videos. Activate," Mr. Meyers said as he continued walking.

"Will do, sir."

Mr. Meyers stopped suddenly and said, "You did get the envelope, right?"

"Yes, I did. I'm going to make the delivery now."

"A lot of people are feeling pain right now, and I don't want anything to jeopardize our mission. Meet me in the control room when you're done with the delivery."

Larry exited the elevator in Global Media Sources' parking garage. Walking towards his Honda Accord, he heard the faint sound of footsteps. He started to walk quickly.

Dropping the keys to his car on the ground, Larry quickly bent down to get them. When he stood up, a tall muscular man appeared behind him.

"Larry Shepherd?" the man asked.

Hesitating to answer, he turned around and responded, "Yes. Who are you?"

"Big Mike sent me to see you. He says you have something for him."

"I was on my way to see Big Mike."

"He wants to keep his communications with you limited. He sent me to get the package."

"How do I know Big Mike sent you?" Larry asked.

"You don't. But I'm here to collect what you have, regardless of whether you believe me or not," the man said as he raised his shirt to reveal the handle of a gun.

"It's in my car."

Larry opened his car door and retrieved a large brown envelope from his glove box, then handed it to the man.

"Tell Big Mike we have more work for him to coordinate. Adding some assassinations and kidnappings to the list."

"I'll let him know."

The man walked away, using the stairs that exited to the street level.

Flustered, Larry went back inside the building. Phase One of Project My Access Chip was about to advance to the next level. A secretary ran towards Larry, stopping him as he approached the elevators.

"Mr. Shepherd, Bone Esquire is holding for you on line one at my desk."

Larry walked to the reception desk and picked up the phone. "What's happening, Bone?"

"Hi, Mr. Shepherd. We just heard about the American Airways Boeing 777 that crashed in New York's Hudson River. Mr. Mole believes his producer was on the plane. Do you have any information about survivors?"

"Tell Mole there are no survivors. This plane crash was intentional and deliberate, and there will be many more. Use the producer's death to strengthen the message in your music to get chipped."

Larry abruptly hung up the telephone.

In the control room, Larry gave Cho a flash drive and instructions from Mr. Meyers on the content that needed to be aired during the breaking news broadcast segments.

"What is this?" Cho asked.

"Information about the chip that Mr. Meyers wants broadcasted during the commercial breaks."

"I haven't reviewed it," Cho said.

"And you don't need to review it."

"I'm not broadcasting something I haven't reviewed. I'll be back," Cho said as he walked off.

Larry placed his hand on Cho's shoulder, pulling him back while turning him around.

"Sorry to disappoint you, Mr. Cho. You don't get a choice on whether or not something gets aired," Larry said forcibly, pointing his finger in Cho's face. "I'd hate to tell Mr. Meyers you're being insubordinate. Especially since he speaks so highly of you."

Cho fiercely slapped Larry's finger and grabbed his neck.

"Don't ever touch me again," Cho said, breathing hard.

Larry frantically shook his neck free of Cho's hand, then started to rub it as Cho rushed away.

In his office, Cho began to review the footage on the flash drive, which displayed a made-for-TV video with wording and images promoting the My Access Chip:

"A parent with Alzheimer's, a spouse who suffers with seizures, a lost child, a family member aboard a plane that crashes or disappears, your police officer husband who's responded to protests against racism that have erupted into a riot…eliminate your worries of safety, whereabouts, mortality…the 'My Access

Chip' is the only way to combat the unknown. Visit www.myaccesschip.com for locations to get your access today."

Another TV video message from Senator Nathaniel Johnson stated, "The greatest development in technology is here. The *My Access Chip*. There's a long list of progressive organizers who have worked diligently behind the scenes to make sure our country and other countries have the technology, not only to protect you and your families, but also to make life easier. Meet me on Friday, February 20th, at six o'clock in the evening at the Foundation Center on Merry Oaks Drive to find out more about this revolutionary device. Be one of the first three hundred people to get chipped for free. For more information, simply visit www.myaccesship.com."

Cho was horrified by what he was viewing.

Larry was in the control room with Mr. Meyers, watching anchor Jenny Purdue. It was nine o'clock in the evening, and she was beginning to speak on the set.

"Here in the nation's capital, there has been a bombing at the Smithshire Historic Hotel on 16th Street."

A view of the area surrounding the hotel was aired, depicting crowds of people with fear in their eyes, hollering and wandering around in the streets. Area restaurants, shopping centers, and other businesses had been evacuated. The sounds of sirens screamed loudly. Policemen were exiting their patrol cars. Emergency personnel were running back and forth. Rescue workers and medical personnel had arrived and were on hand to assist hotel staff, guests, and spectators. Police officers restricted access to more and more of the areas around the hotel.

Jenny continued her report, "We've received information that several people are injured and there have been some fatalities. The Smithshire is one of the oldest luxury hotels in D.C., dating back to the early 1900s. I'm getting a report that reporter Drew Shaw has a hotel guest with him now who was injured."

"Hi, Jenny," Shaw said excitedly. "I'm here at the end of 16th Street with Ben Brackens."

"Is he okay?" Jenny asked.

"He has some cuts and bruises, but he'll be okay," Drew replied.

The middle-aged man appeared in the camera, looking distraught and shaken, with an expression of fright in his eyes.

Jenny began to talk to him. "Where are you from?"

He began to whisper a comment, "Me and my wife and two kids are visiting here from Spokane, Washington."

"Where are your wife and kids?"

"They're with the paramedics."

"Are they okay?"

"Yes."

"Can you tell us what happened?" Jenny asked.

He nodded slowly.

"We were standing in the restaurant lobby, getting ready to take the elevator to our room. We had just finished eating dinner. Without warning, the hotel's restaurant ignited into a burning furnace. My family and I were lucky because we were near the entrance of the building. We were able to get down the stone steps with a herd of other guests. I know we'd be dead if we'd been anywhere else in the hotel," the man said as tears began to roll down his face.

"Did you see anything suspicious prior to the explosion?" Jenny asked.

"No," the man said, his voice trembling.

As the man was talking, the camera zoomed in on a young woman with bandages around her head sitting inside an ambulance.

"According to the police chief, there are terrorists at large in the city. The public is urged to act with caution and remain calm," Drew said. "They're dealing with the unknown. Where are they from? How many? We don't know as of yet. The FBI, Secret Service, CIA, and a multitude of other law enforcement agencies are involved."

Mr. Meyers looked at Larry with a shrewd smile. "A herd of other guests? Really? I'm thinking they would have been trampled, had it been a herd. Yes, they were lucky," he said.

"Okay, Drew. Thank you," Jenny said. "We've got reporter Megan Sullivan on the scene in New York, ready to report on the plane crash."

"The president is urging people to remain calm. The CIA, FBI, and other federal agencies are on the ground, investigating the theory of terrorists. There have been a chain of incidents occurring within an hour of one another. We're getting reports of other hotel bombings and plane crashes," Megan said.

The camera followed her as she moved through the crowd.

It was a Wednesday night Bible study at Triumphant Baptist Church. Pastor McFarland was preparing to discuss biblical scriptures in the book of Revelations related to the seven stars and seven lampstands. Luke and members of the congregation were seated in the church cafeteria with their Bibles opened to the book of Revelations.

Because of the seriousness of what was being shown on the news, Luke had asked his pastor if they could turn on the TV.

The faces captured by the camera reflected pure, mesmerized terror. People all over the world were asked to take normal safety measures and remain calm as further investigations of the incidents took place.

"Through the Apostle John, Jesus dictated letters for communication to seven handpicked churches located throughout Asia Minor. The letters were His attempt to warn the people about the consequences of their wrongdoings, that they needed to wake up and repent. You can't begin to imagine the wrath that those who turn away from God will encounter," Pastor McFarland said softly as everyone sat watching the TV.

CHAPTER 5

A day later, *The Washington Herald* had a picture on its cover page that depicted an invasion of terrorists laying bombs throughout cities where the hotel bombings had occurred. The caption at the top of the image read: "Where are they now?"

Jenny was back on the air to do an early morning report. "The government and law enforcement agencies are on top of the hotel bombings and plane crashes. It's believed all of the incidents are connected. How do we protect ourselves in the future? The 'Right Now! Right Time! Chip'. Now is the time for everyone to get chipped."

Cho and Malin were sitting at their breakfast table, watching the early morning news. Malin placed a bowl of cereal in front of Cho.

"The Chip!" Malin shouted. "Adrika's doctor had a chip inserted in her."

"What?" Cho yelled out. "What do you mean he had the chip inserted in her?"

Hesitating, a little confused by Cho's reaction, Malin said, "She got it a couple months ago. I remember trying to call you to get your thoughts while we were at the doctor's office, but you didn't answer your cell phone. I never really thought about it again. The doctor said it was a medical device that would be beneficial due to her medical situation."

"Malin, the chip is what Pastor McFarland has been discussing for the past several months."

"What are you talking about? He's never mentioned anything about a chip."

"Yes, the My Access Chip, Malin."

"Sorry, honey, I didn't make the connection when the doctor talked about her getting it for patient safety and identification purposes."

"That's the sales pitch they're using."

"Why doesn't the government do something? I'm sure our new president wouldn't support the chip if it was bad for us."

Cho looked at Malin strongly and said, "It's the government who's in collaboration with my company and iTrack!"

"That can't be. The government protects us."

"I assure you, the government is very involved with the chip — and make no mistake about it, they're willing to do what's necessary to make sure everyone gets chipped."

"Do you think they're responsible for the bombings and plane crashes?"

Cho responded, "There are so many secret hands in the pot, you just don't know who to trust. I do know that whatever's in the works, it's about to go full force. I'd better get to work."

"Aren't you worried? If you're right about your company, aren't you worried?"

"I'll be okay. I need to control my emotions until I can figure out some things. Don't you worry about me."

"You're my husband. It's my job to worry if you might be in harm's way."

As Cho walked towards the front door, Malin shouted out, "Don't forget about Pastor McFarland's book signing tonight at the church. He'll be signing copies of the new book *Power of the Pastor: The Good, Bad, and Ugly*."

"I definitely plan on being there."

Cho and his family had been members of Triumphant Baptist Church for nearly twenty years. They were a part of the initial twelve worshippers who started the church in Pastor McFarland's living room. Due to the growth of their congregation to 5,000 members, the pastor and church leaders had been instrumental in the purchase of three worship facilities. Now, in their second phase of the pastor's Vision 2030 Campaign, he was planning for another new facility that would accommodate more than 8,000 members by the year 2030.

Later that evening, Matt Meyers, Sam Walker, and Larry Shepherd received text notifications that Mr. Denmart, chairman and CEO of Global Media Sources, was in Dallas and wanted to meet with them at nine o'clock the following morning. The meeting location was his President's Suite at the Executive Mansion on Turtle Creek Drive. The pressure for getting more and more people chipped was about to be increased. Mr. Denmart wanted to discuss those who had been handpicked to further the movement and outline their assignments.

Larry was the first to arrive at the Executive Mansion. Security personnel directed him to the special elevators. From there, he was escorted by the concierge to the 70th floor. When they arrived, the concierge rang the doorbell. Mr. Denmart opened the door, dressed casually. Larry was impressed with the layout of the room. At a glance, he saw it was equipped with marble tile flooring, elegant wood furnishings, a state of the art kitchen and bar, and a rooftop terrace with a stunning view of Dallas.

"Welcome to my suite," Mr. Denmart said. "Have a seat."

"This is really nice, Mr. Denmart," Larry said as he sat down at a big round conference table.

Mr. Denmart moved to sit on a sofa across from the table. "Before the others get here, I want to commend you for the work you've done thus far."

"Just doing my part to further the movement."

"I must say I'm sorely disappointed with Cho and his lack of support."

Larry responded, "With all the company has done for him and his family, you'd think his loyalty would be greater. Frankly, I never trusted him."

Mr. Denmart nodded and said, "If his loyalty doesn't turn around, the consequences for not doing so will be severe."

Trying to control his impatience, Mr. Denmart glanced and commented on the timeliness of both Matt Meyers and Sam Walker; it was 9:01 am. Larry started to look nervous and uneasy.

"The cascade of incidents yesterday are just for starters. You're with the upper crust, Shepherd, and as such, there's no turning back. From the top, we move, and we move hard and heavy with no consideration of the impact on those underneath us."

Larry nodded and uttered a nervous laugh.

"I'm sorry, Shepherd, I neglected to offer you something to drink. Water? Bourbon? Cognac?"

"I'm good, sir."

"If you need or want anything, just let me know."

The doorbell rang. It was Matt Meyers and Sam Walker. The two men entered, then they all situated themselves at the conference table.

"I want to first talk about the visit to the distribution plant in Louisiana, then the meeting with Natas, the plane crashes, and the bombings, the push by government officials to move our agenda full throttle. It's time the persons we've handpicked start moving forward with their assignments. To gain another three-point-something billion implants over the next six months, our pressure to convince must be severe."

The gentlemen stared intensely at Mr. Denmart as he continued.

"How do we convince the masses to get chipped? We do so through our strategy of creating anxiety to justify the need for governmental control at home and tactical warfare overseas. This strategy includes the deployment of increased catastrophic homegrown and terrorist events, and we'll start with the most exciting city on Earth — New York City!"

Their eyes widened with big, cheeky grins.

Mr. Meyers reached in his workbag. "We may as well go ahead and pull out our iTrackPads. Mr. Denmart's secretary sent us the information regarding Phase I of Project My Access Chip."

He waited for his device to power on.

"Shepherd, you've done a great job working with your team on targeted video ads," Mr. Denmart said, "but we'll need much more than TV messages. We need PR and social media gurus on the ground night and day. Not just TV; we need campaigns that extend from emails, text messages, billboards, newspapers, bulletins, commercials to websites, and telephones that address every facet of one's life. From the single mother trying to keep a roof over the heads of her and kids, to the single mother who wants to go back to college. From the wannabe entrepreneur, to the we-can-make-you a six-figure businessman. The message is simple: 'All you need to do is get chipped.'"

Sam interjected, "Mr. Denmart, we need more than just people skilled in PR and social media. We need folks with those skills who endorse and support the mission."

"Absolutely," Mr. Denmart confirmed.

Sam continued. "We need to find those individuals who yearn for significance. To make a difference. Who want to belong and contribute and be a part of something so big, they can be swayed to do anything we ask of them."

"Right. How can we appeal to that fundamental need to belong and contribute?" Mr. Denmart asked. "That's the question."

"We need a draw. A pull to get the right fit of people who want their names, interests, and/or talents associated with something significant," Larry said calmly. "The more delusional they are, the more devoted they'll be to us and the mission. Modern day sacrificial lambs."

"Sacrificial lambs…I like that. But we need a more marketable word, like 'Engagers'. That's what we'll call them," Mr. Denmart said with excitement. "They'll be the people on the ground reaching the masses with the various communication tools. With the partnerships we now have with virtually every industry, we can use them to further our agenda to communicate our messages to their recipients and consumers. They'll be vital to pulling people into something they don't want to do or something they haven't thought about doing. At some point, the 'Engagers' must be willing to be the sacrificial lambs to get the point across."

"I'll start working on finding our modern day sacrificial lambs, the 'Engagers', Mr. Denmart," Larry said.

"Great!"

"In reviewing the four focal points for Phase I, which include medical facilities, financial institutions, churches, the entertainment industry, and schools, our 'Engagers', along with the handpicked politicians, celebrities, sports figures, and clergy, we'll solidify our targeted demographics in a matter of weeks," Larry said.

"Right," Sam said.

"The product, data centers, and infrastructure for medical personnel to implant the chip are already in place. Mercy

Methodist Hospital and Concord Memorial Hospital and other hospitals, clinics, and emergency care centers throughout the U.S. have established protocols for implantation. All entities have a high number of the capsule on hand. The partners we've recruited from every industry to be tracking stations are now housing electromagnetic readers on site. We now have in place solid infrastructures to manufacture, deliver, store, implant, transmit, read, respond, and transact."

"Now, let's take a look at religious, political, community, and celebrity influencers," Mr. Denmart said.

"Yes, sir," Larry responded.

Mr. Meyers said, "We have two groups out there with enormous influence. Luckily for us, the one with the largest following is supportive of getting chipped."

"Yes, your Pastor Dobbs has already taken the first step and gotten himself and his family chipped," Mr. Denmart said.

"And he's gotten other prominent pastors throughout the U.S. to follow his lead," Larry assured.

"Great!" Mr. Denmart exclaimed.

"Senator Johnson's meeting at the Foundation Center will be huge," Larry commented. "Being one of the youngest senators, he has a huge following all throughout this country. Social media has been essential to him gaining such popularity."

"Great!" Mr. Denmart said. "Natas has agreed to come to town for that meeting."

"Then there's Pastor McFarland, who I have security surveillance on," Sam announced.

"Yes, he's definitely a problem that'll eventually need to be dealt with," Mr. Meyers confirmed. "Plus, he has that new book out that contradicts everything about our movement."

"Don't worry about him and his new book," Sam reassured. "We'll deal with him like we did Dr. Millsap."

"Let's just focus on Pastor Dobbs and his influence. As you can see on your iTrackPad, over the next two months we'll be visiting with pastors throughout the U.S. about getting chipped and then encouraging their members to get chipped," Mr. Meyers stated. "Along with these scheduled visits, we'll be working with local and national medical facilities on disseminating information about TrueCare Health Reform, the benefits of enrollment, and the incentives for getting chipped."

"Of course, we'll start with Louisiana and the other southern states," Mr. Denmart said.

"Shepherd, I need you to get on top of the interview with Pastor Dobbs. We need his message to be spotlighted on all our media outlets."

"I've already scheduled him for an interview with Ms. Walker for our TrueAccess Magazine."

"Great!" Mr. Denmart said. "Can she be trusted?"

"Yes, sir. I handpicked her myself. She's a recent addition to the Global family and very eager to please her superiors."

Larry cast an anxious glance at Mr. Denmart, waiting for his reaction.

Insistently, Mr. Denmart continued. "There's a Dr. Irene Cooper becoming very vocal on the cable networks about the chip being a control device that's been created to destroy our current way of life. She's talking about the numbering of every living creature, the numbering of every tangible item, and the tracking of such through databases and computer systems, which according to her will impact one's freedom and privacy. She's leading the opposition."

Mr. Meyers interrupted him, "This is definitely not the sort of negative information we want shared."

"She's on our radar as well," Sam assured.

"She's making people think they won't be able to communicate freely with one another and that their every conversation and activity will be monitored and tracked," Mr. Denmart said.

"We all know that's true, but we don't want people thinking that way," Larry said, laughing.

"That's why it's so important for people of prominence and influence to dispel that negativity to their followers and then help us sway people who are uncertain about the chip," Mr. Denmart said.

"The 'Engagers' can be very important with this initiative as they develop messages to be disseminated through our defined communication tools," Larry said.

"Definitely."

"If it comes to it, she'll disappear like Dr. Millsap," Larry assured.

They were interrupted by the ringing of the doorbell. Mr. Denmart got up to go answer the door, and when he opened it, there stood the concierge and five workers from Angie's Bakery. The concierge and bakery workers walked in and began to set up an array of breakfast items Mr. Denmart had ordered for the meeting.

Larry attempted to continue their discussion, but Mr. Denmart looked at Larry and shushed him. Waiting for the staff to finish, Larry looked at Mr. Denmart apologetically. The servers finally finished and quietly exited the room. Mr. Denmart closed the door and turned quickly to invite the gentlemen to partake of the breakfast items.

Scanning his iTrackPad, Mr. Denmart saw what he was looking for. "Larry, tell me about these celebrity rappers, Bone Esquire and Mo Money Monte."

Larry wanted to keep his relationship with Mo Money Monte concealed but knew it was time for him to reveal that Mo Money

Monte was his son. Larry maneuvered his way back to the conference table and sat down with his food.

Letting out an audible gasp, Larry began to talk. "First, I must admit that Ivan Shepherd, known as Mo Money Monte, is my biological son. He was conceived when I was a very young man. Due to his mother's hatred for me, I've never been able to have a relationship with him. I am by no means a deadbeat dad and have supported him financially from childbirth. Because of his name change, I wasn't aware that my son was a premier rapper. Most of my involvement with the music entertainment was with gospel. It wasn't until my wife was concerned about our fifteen-year-old son, Jeremy's, interest in rapping and his following of Bone Esquire that I started to do my homework."

Mr. Denmart and the faces of the others were unreadable. Larry kept talking in a nervous tone.

"After seeing the influence Bone Esquire had on Jeremy and his friends, I knew he would be essential for the movement."

Cutting him off with a look, Mr. Denmart said, "Again, what is your relationship with Mo Money Monte now?"

"Like I said, sir, he's my son. I'm in the process of connecting with him," Larry responded. "He's currently in jail on a bad rap. I've contacted my attorneys about taking his case."

Mr. Denmart got up and walked calmly into the kitchen area, where he opened the refrigerator to get a bottle of water. Clutching the bottle tightly, he said, "The one thing I will not tolerate is someone who lies to me. You can lie on my behalf, but not to me."

Mr. Meyers and Sam turned to stare at each other. From the look on Mr. Denmart's face and the vibes he started to display, they were able to discern that he wasn't happy. Sensing the same, Larry gave Mr. Meyers and Sam a panicked glance.

Mr. Denmart snapped, "Do I look like a stupid man to you, Larry?" His voice was rushed, and his demeanor progressed to volatile.

Sam almost choked on a sip of water he'd just taken.

Larry responded quietly, "No, sir."

"Do I look like a dumb or naïve man to you, Larry?" Mr. Denmart said, a little calmer.

Larry responded again, quietly, "No, sir." The meeting had taken a different direction than what Larry had envisioned.

Mr. Denmart began to tap his pen on the table as he reared back in his chair. He thought for a moment, then said, "You don't get to become the chairman and CEO of a company like Global Media Sources, the world's largest media and entertainment conglomerate, employing over 50,000 employees worldwide, without being smart, wise, straightforward, a levelheaded risk taker, a catalyst for high expectations, a visionary who sees the next great opportunity, and one who surrounds himself with talented individuals who deliver perfection and achievement of the highest quality. With all that being said, I have to know who I have sitting next to me. And right now, I have a liar sitting next to me. And it's you, Larry Shepherd!"

Larry looked horrified. He knew his own personal disaster was about to erupt.

"Those sitting next to me, my talented employees, don't lie to me," Mr. Denmart stated. "Before I even considered you, Larry, for such a key role in this movement, I had your background, your wife's background, and your mother-in-law's background investigated. I know about your relationship with Irene Mascot, your illegitimate son's mother. I know Mo Money Monte's been your little hidden secret since his birth and that your wife and family have no knowledge of him. I know you never wanted a relationship with him. I even know about your daughters, both of whom you're using for our movement. Now, how do you propose I move forward with someone who's just lied to me? Your extramarital affairs are of no direct concern to me, nor are any intimate details of your life."

The impact of Denmart's calm, quiet question was shattering. Larry stared at him with fear, then he spoke, as if almost paralyzed. "Please forgive me, Mr. Denmart. More than anything, I am loyal to you, this company, and this movement. I would never want to disappoint you. For so long, I've carried the shame of having children from outside relationships, matters that would have caused me not to become a deacon in any church or a respected community leader."

"I even know about the time you broke your wife's arm," Denmart added.

With a look of defeat, Larry placed his face in his hands. The faces of Mr. Meyers and Sam reeked of astonishment. With their eyes glued to their iTrackPads, they remained silent while processing the enormity of what they'd heard, as well as the fear of disclosure about their own personal lives.

"My intent was only to share the facts of what I know about you, and there's more. It is of no concern to me how you run your household, nor how you treat your wife. But the thought that you would use any deceptive practices against me, Global Media Sources, iTrack, Inc., and the movement is my concern. I have no use for deceivers or pretenders," Mr. Denmart stressed.

Larry raised his face and with frantic eyes said, "Mr. Denmart, I promise you can count on me. I, myself, will be a sacrificial lamb."

Mr. Meyers and Sam stared blankly at one another.

"It's my understanding that your son has been trying to reach out to you. His involvement with Bone Esquire is critical. The two of them together have a huge influence on a population that can be easily persuaded to get chipped."

"I will get in touch with him," Larry said as he struggled to gather his emotions.

"In prison, he's joined forces with Pastor McFarland, and he's planning to release a Christian rap album," Mr. Denmart said. "All of that must be stopped, or his prison stay will be prolonged. I thought about having him killed, but he's more valuable to us alive than dead. That is, if he complies."

"I understand, sir."

"I'm not sure how successful the stabbing was," Mr. Denmart shared.

"Stabbing?" Larry asked.

"Yes. Stabbing," Mr. Denmart responded. "Just know that you need to return his call and get close to him."

Mr. Meyers interrupted and said, "We're moving forward with Bone Esquire kicking off the My Access Keeper blog."

"We also have *The Pledge Access Concert Tour* series getting ready to start. Your son needs to be onboard with the movement. He'll be a part of the lineup with Bone Esquire as soon as he gets out of jail. The tour is scheduled to start next month," Mr. Denmart said. "With the acquisition and launching of our music streaming service, and what we'll slate as their unity tour, we'll also tout them as artist-owned music streaming moguls. The title everyone will be hash tagging will be #Alpha&OmegaMafiaMyChipAccessforAll."

"Ingenious," Sam said.

"Right. It'll generate so many revenue streams for them and other artists. Everyone will want to be connected at any cost."

"August 2021 will be here before we realize it. There's a lot of planning and executing that needs to take place."

"I understand, Mr. Denmart," Larry agreed. "What I would ask, sir, is that if his release can be expedited. I need him out of prison now to work on him."

"Consider it done," Mr. Denmart assured.

"We also need a team of 'Engagers' on the ground immediately to manage the posting and monitoring of all our social media forums. A young person who will live, eat, and breathe the social media tools," Mr. Denmart emphasized, "and someone we can trust with certain confidential matters."

"Absolutely," Mr. Meyers agreed. "Social networking has become the new way of sharing and getting advice related to mental, emotional, social, and psychological needs. We can definitely capitalize on that."

"We're on it," Larry said.

"By the way, how are you enjoying that CL Coupe?" Mr. Denmart asked.

Larry smiled. "That is one fine Mercedes. I probably didn't need to get the heated wood/leather steering wheel, but I couldn't resist. I'm an executive producer now. All my options ran my cost up to $260,000."

"You deserve it for all you've done thus far for Project My Access Chip," Denmart assured him. "What you've done behind the scenes is invaluable. I expect to have no concerns associated with your lying. I expect the union between you and your son to be a top priority. We need him, and we need him now. If persuasion needs to be forced, then do whatever is necessary."

"Yes, sir."

"Update us quickly on the 'By Invitation Only' campaign," Mr. Denmart insisted.

"We've obtained email addresses from the account holders of various companies and institutions. We've kicked off the email campaign 'By Invitation Only', and we've gotten a great response."

Mr. Denmart interjected, "I know. People love to share their thoughts on the products and services of major companies."

Larry directed everyone's attention to a link on their iTrackPads that displayed a sample email showing a collage of various pictures representing a family's daily activities: eating in a restaurant, at work, at school, at a baseball game, at an outdoor concert. The caption underneath said, 'You're passionate about your family and what keeps them happy and safe. So we want to hear and learn from you. We're proud to introduce this exclusive opportunity to speak your mind. As our thanks to you, you and five family members can get chipped for free! Simply sign up. Share your thoughts. We'll send you a free gift to get chipped. In three simple steps, you'll be on your way to getting your free My Access Chip! It's easy, safe, and best of all, offers protection for you and your family.'"

"Nice," Mr. Denmart stated.

"I like the relationships you've been diligently working to build with our service and business partners. The downloadable app that allows people to share has been a hit."

CHAPTER 6

The time had come for Pastor Dobbs to increase his activities to sway his followers to get chipped. His church, True Christian Followers, was one of the fastest growing churches in the Dallas area. Within seventeen years, the charismatic forty-year-old had grown the church's membership from 43 to over 8,000. Having ties as a social services activist, his influence transcended all communities.

Larry had scheduled an interview with TrueAccess Magazine so the pastor could begin the first phase of connecting to and engaging his followers to get chipped. Pastor Dobbs had asked Larry to meet him at an apartment he had at the Historic Crestmont Apartments, located in Downtown Dallas. They would visit with the magazine reporter there to ensure privacy.

"Hello, Pastor," Larry said to Pastor Dobbs as he walked into his apartment. It was nine o'clock in the morning. "Did I wake you?"

"No, I'm up," Pastor Dobbs responded as he flipped a switch to turn on the lights. Walking slowly into the kitchen area, he asked, "I have a pot of coffee brewing. Would you like a cup?"

"No, sir. I've had my cup for the day," Larry said, walking behind him.

Pastor Dobbs, with an athletic build, was wearing a Ralph Lauren black cashmere robe.

"What time did you tell the reporter to arrive?"

"This morning at 9:30, Pastor."

Larry paused as he heard movement in the bedroom area. He hesitated thoughtfully for a moment and then asked, "Is First Lady Dobbs with you?"

"No, a friend stopped by. She'll stay in the room until we're finished."

Larry remained silent and sat in a chair at the bar.

Fixing his coffee, Pastor Dobbs turned to Larry and said, "We're at a crucial point in the movement now. With the incidents that occurred the other day, we have the perfect opportunity to start helping people think more seriously about safety precautions and ways to protect themselves and their loved ones."

"Yes, the cold, frozen fear we witnessed in the eyes and voices of the people at the hotel in D.C. and those impacted by the plane crash in New York have people listening."

"It helps that we sent members of our congregation to the D.C. area for the Baptist Convention, some of whom were staying at that hotel."

"What was the final death count for your members who were at the hotel when the bombing occurred?"

"Eleven. We're having funeral services for five family members on Saturday."

"Wonderful."

"Yes. Another opportunity for me to talk about doing whatever is necessary to keep Americans safe, and to encourage their loved ones, neighbors, co-workers, and friends to make a commitment to get chipped."

"Yes," Larry echoed while looking at the bedroom door.

"Let me go get presentable for the reporter from TrueAccess Magazine. Thinking I'll sport that $2,000 Canali suit and my $700 Gucci loafers today," Pastor Dobbs said proudly.

"Looking forward to the day," Larry said, laughing. "Remember, we're going to keep the interview simple."

Pastor Dobbs nodded in agreement and left the room.

Thirty minutes later, a knock at the door interrupted Pastor Dobbs' conversation with Larry. Pastor Dobbs moved swiftly to open the door, wearing his blue, fitted Canali suit.

Jasmine Walker, a very pretty, curvy African-American woman with a short, naturally curly hairstyle who was in her mid-thirties, stood in the doorway, waiting to be greeted. Pastor Dobbs invited her in. She walked in with an air of supreme confidence, dressed expensively in a cap-sleeve, fitted, chocolate tweed dress, Stuart Weitzman pumps, and tinted Gucci glasses.

Larry stood up and started to walk towards her.

"Hi, Jasmine. This is my pastor, Pastor Dobbs of True Christian Followers," Larry said to introduce the two. He turned to Pastor Dobbs. "She's one of our most talented reporters."

"And I'm sure your prettiest reporter," Pastor Dobbs said, smiling.

She smiled, and with a bob of her head she reached out to shake the pastor's hand. As their hands touched, her brown eyes locked with Pastor Dobbs'. He responded by complimenting her beauty and offering to sit her purse down for her. Her golden brown cheeks became red with a mixture of embarrassment and gratitude. Pastor Dobbs invited her to have a seat on the sofa. Larry sat in a chair across from her.

"Can I offer you a cup of coffee, tea, or wine?" Pastor Dobbs asked.

"I'll take a glass or bottle of water," Jasmine responded graciously as she removed her glasses.

"Great!" Pastor Dobbs said as he walked in the kitchen to retrieve a bottle of water.

"We can go ahead and get started with the interview," Larry stated.

"It's definitely a pleasure to meet you, Pastor Dobbs," Jasmine said as she watched the pastor retrieve a bottle of water from the refrigerator.

"No, the pleasure is all mine, Ms. Walker," Pastor Dobbs said, handing her the bottle and sitting on the sofa next to her.

"Thank you." She noticed a slight bulge of skin on the pastor's right hand. "I've heard such wonderful things about you and all that you're doing in the community."

Pastor Dobbs sensed her stare and returned it, and for a second his smile widened and his eyes sparkled.

"Jasmine, I know you've already done your research and know my pastor is a native of Dallas and that he holds a BA degree in Psychology from Howard Mills University, a Master's of Divinity degree from the University of Texas, and he's currently working on his second doctoral degree," Larry stated.

Jasmine pulled out her laptop and turned it on. Her fingers were poised to type anything Pastor Dobbs might say.

"Yes, I'm aware of Pastor Dobbs' background. In 2006, he received his Doctorate of Ministry degree from Southwestern Baptist Theological Seminary. He founded True Christian Followers in 2004, and in seventeen years he's grown his membership from 43 to over 8,000. One of the youngest progressive ministers in the city. And his focus on the homeless has gained nationwide attention."

"And even more impressive, I'm almost at 80,000 followers on iAccessagram," Pastor Dobbs said with a smile.

"What I want to talk to you about today is your support of the My Access Chip," Jasmine clarified. "Now, do you have the implantable chip?"

"I believe you noticed it earlier," Pastor Dobbs said as he extended his right hand.

"I know you're a huge proponent of the chip, which many of your counterparts have tagged as the Antichrist," Jasmine said directly. "They say it's an invasion of privacy and the true mission of the device is to track our movements and gain human control."

"If I believed I was supporting the theory of the Antichrist, the Mark of the Beast, I assure you I wouldn't have gotten chipped. I wouldn't have allowed my wife and kids to get chipped. I have an autistic child. After reading a story about an autistic girl who went missing and was found dead three days later, I knew my wife and I needed something more than what we could offer our son in terms of safety. When my youngest child gets on a bus going on a field trip, I don't want to wonder about her status if something happens to that bus. In my ministry work with the homeless and runaway teens, so many people are in pain, agonizing over the whereabouts of loved ones."

"And Pastor, if you were like me as a kid, you more than likely at some point skipped school," Larry said, laughing. "Well, if your kids have the chip, you and school administrators can confirm that your child got off the bus, and where they are located real time."

"And now, for convenience sake, I'm looking forward to the wave of my hand at the grocery store to pay for my goods," Pastor Dobbs stated.

"In this interview, what message do you want to send to our readers about the 'My Access Chip'?" Jasmine asked.

Studying her for a moment, Pastor Dobbs responded, "I had a dream a few years ago about a divine device that would be introduced to the world. This device would provide access to a near perfect life."

Jasmine took a sip of water as she listened to Pastor Dobbs.

"I want your readers to understand that the My Access Chip is not the Mark of the Beast. I've chosen to get it because I know how important it is to have for me and my family as well as how important it'll be for all families, especially those of us with special needs children or aging parents. Not to mention those wondering about the whereabouts of loved ones in the event of a natural disaster, traffic accident, airplane crash, school bombing or a protest that escalates into a riot."

Jasmine interjected, "What do you say to those who claim it's medically dangerous?"

"Ms. Walker, look at my hand," Pastor Dobbs said as he extended it for her to look at, then continued, "does it look dangerous? My goodness, it's as simple as getting a flu vaccine. It's as simple as getting your blood work done at the doctor's office. A needle insertion is required for both."

"What do you say about those who are promoting it as being cool?"

"It's not about being cool; it's about being safe and secure," Pastor Dobbs said.

"How do you respond to the critics who say if you get the chip, you'll die?"

"I say they're misinforming people. Somehow, they've misinterpreted scripture in the Bible. The My Access Chip is about safety, security, and convenience. It's that simple," Pastor Dobbs stressed.

"What is your response to those who say churches like yours are working with the government to influence your members to get chipped, and as a result you're getting kickbacks for doing so?"

"First, I must say those claims are false! Pure and simple!" Pastor Dobbs exclaimed. "Secondly, under my leadership, my congregation has grown from 43 members to 8,000 members in seventeen years. I know the growth has to do with the fact that not only are my teachings rooted in the Gospel, but also my love for people, believers and non-believers both. It shouldn't be surprising that wherever people feel genuine love, they'll come. Like those from our homeless program."

Larry nodded his head in agreement.

"Unfortunately, love is a human emotion that's missing in a lot of lives. My teachings, which always come back to how Jesus first loved us and gave His life for us, serve as an ongoing reminder of our responsibility to love one another in the midst of our circumstances, whatever they may be. Believe me, that has nothing to do with the government."

"I know you have quite a few ministries," Jasmine stated.

"With over 100 ministries and hundreds of ministry workers, we're able to provide an array of programs and services to our members. We have doctors, nurses, attorneys, educators, social workers, human resources professionals, insurance professionals, fitness professionals, business owners, etc. You name the profession, more than likely we have it represented at True Christian Followers. And our members either head up or work in the various ministries. In addition, with 20% of the 8,000 members paying tithes consistently, we're able to really benefit the community. As stated before, none of our programs and services, ranging from job training workshops, home buying seminars, health and career fairs, to entrepreneurial workshops, have anything to do with the government."

As Pastor Dobbs responded to Jasmine's questions, Larry sat back, thinking about the next steps they'd need to activate to further the movement.

"Last Sunday, I visited your church and really enjoyed the service," Jasmine admitted.

"I hate I wasn't aware of your attendance," Pastor Dobbs said with a smile.

"It was a last minute decision," Jasmine said, then continued, "I noticed that after the ten o'clock morning service, there were individuals on the premises to sign your members up for the new health care program. How did you get involved in that?"

Pastor Dobbs hesitated for a long, thoughtful moment and said, "As I stated, we have a number of our members heading up various ministries, such as our health care ministry. Because we know a huge number of our members don't have health care insurance, we wanted to work with the local hospitals to give our members direct access to information about affordable insurance and the ability to sign up. Many of our members aren't well educated about affordable insurance, nor do they have computers at home."

"I see," Jasmine responded. "How do you respond when your critics say you're working with the government to influence your members to get the implantable chip?"

"Again, I would say I'm not working with the government. I got the chip primarily for safety and security purposes, and I encourage my members to do so for the same reasons."

Jasmine smiled and said, "How do you respond to critics of the Health Care Reform Act who say a section of the bill talks about a Class II device? And the theory is the language, although vague, opens the gate for making the implantable device that's referenced in the bill mandatory for all U.S. citizens?"

"I read the language people are referring to in the bill. The implantable device is only referenced in the context of patient identification and health information."

"Tell the readers about your new community center. Your critics are saying it was built with money you received from the government in exchange for your support of the My Access Chip," Jasmine stated sternly.

Larry deliberately interrupted to inform Jasmine that Pastor Dobbs had another pending meeting he needed to get ready for.

"All I'll say is that we're good stewards of the money we receive from tithes and offerings. It was sound financial and strategic planning that brought to fruition a long-term vision to benefit the community we serve."

"Have you heard about Pastor McFarland's new book, *Power of the Pastor: The Good, Bad, and Ugly*?" Jasmine asked.

"Yes, I've heard about it. And no, I haven't read it. I have no need to read it," Pastor Dobbs emphasized. "He's been a long-term, vocal critic of mine. In case you didn't know, there's jealousy among pastors. He's been a pastor for over twenty years. I've nearly doubled the size of his membership."

Jasmine smiled at Pastor Dobbs' last comment and said, "In his book, he implies that the government is courting pastors like you. That the government is awarding you financially for encouraging your members to get chipped."

"Totally untrue, Ms. Walker."

Larry stood up and said, "Jasmine, Pastor Dobbs must get ready for his next meeting."

Jasmine gave Larry a quick look and said, "I understand. Pastor Dobbs, I'll move forward with publishing your interview; however, I'd like us to schedule a follow-up interview. I'd also like to get your thoughts on the movement for a one world government."

"I'll certainly look forward to indulging you on that subject matter, Ms. Walker. It'll be critical for ending global division," Pastor Dobbs said as he stood and retrieved her purse. "I am so thankful you took the time to interview me."

"It was definitely my pleasure," Jasmine said as she put on her glasses and proceeded to walk towards the door.

Feeling the men watching her, she turned and smiled inexplicably back at them, then waited for Pastor Dobbs to open the door for her.

"Larry will work on a date to reschedule. I'll definitely look forward to visiting with you again," Pastor Dobbs said, smiling. "And I'll definitely look forward to reading your article."

"Oh, before I forget, will you be at Senator Johnson's meeting tomorrow evening?" Jasmine asked.

"Yes, I do plan on being there."

"Great! Maybe I'll see you there," Jasmine said as she walked away.

"I sure hope so."

Pastor Dobbs returned to the living room, where Larry was waiting. He looked confidently at Larry and said, "I'm looking forward to getting to know that young lady better."

Larry smiled.

A day later, Senator Johnson stood at the entrance of the Foundation Center, greeting the attendees as they arrived. In the heart of Downtown Dallas, the center, known for its upscale and versatile space, world-class service, and genuine Texas elegance, was the perfect location for the meeting. The theater-style venue had a seating capacity of 2,000. Invitations had been sent to more than one hundred leaders throughout the surrounding communities. Many were curious about the meeting, but Senator Johnson had limited his disclosure of the fine details.

While Senator Johnson was in the midst of talking to and greeting the individuals coming through the front entrance, Mr. Denmart, Pastor Dobbs, House Representative Smith and Jim Natas were being escorted through a back entrance. They were directed by Senator Johnson's staff to sit on the front row.

Senator Johnson opened the meeting and said, "Greetings, family, friends, constituents, and supporters. I'm so grateful for your attendance this evening. Before I get started, I would like to acknowledge some special guests of mine in the audience, Mr. Denmart of Global Media Sources, Pastor Dobbs of True Christian Followers, House Representative Tadd Smith, and Jim Natas of iTrack, Inc."

The people in the audience weren't familiar with the names of Mr. Denmart or Jim Natas, but they started to clap their hands.

"When I ran for office three years ago, at the top of my list of priorities I promised I would pursue innovative ways to move our country forward. From the lowest unemployment rate to our kids graduating from colleges in higher numbers, working with foreign counterparts around the world to safeguard our Earth and make sure future generations have a safe place to call home, to leading a fight to make our world supreme again."

A round of applause started as Senator Johnson continued to speak.

"This country has thrived on the advancement of technology, but what I want to speak about here this evening is a creation that will revolutionize your lives. I know it's revolutionized my life. That revolutionary technology is inside my right hand."

Senator Johnson raised his right hand for everyone in the audience to see.

"This tiny piece of technology will make all nations supreme!"

Senator Johnson paused a moment to glance at his special guests.

"I know some of you are wondering about the safety of having a device implanted inside you. Health concerns? No worries; insertion is easy. You don't feel a thing. What'll be implanted inside of you is about the size of a kernel of corn."

Senator Johnson paused again, trying the study the reaction of the people in the audience.

"Now, I must be honest with you. There are a number of individuals against the chip. As a matter of fact, there's a group down the street having their own meeting this evening. A meeting to discredit this creation. Despite what you may have heard on TV or read in the press, the chip's sole purpose is to create a greater and better way of life for all."

People in the crowd stood and began to raise signs they'd been given and chanted, "My free chip, my free chip, my free chip."

Senator Johnson nodded in acknowledgement and waved his hands to calm the crowd. He said, "No, we haven't forgotten. You were informed that the first three hundred attendees would be chipped for free. But, there has been a change. And that change is that everyone in attendance this evening will be chipped for free."

The crowd started to cheer Senator Johnson's name. Volunteers came forward to help calm the crowd down. Senator Johnson's staffers had secured several rooms in the back of the Foundation Center. Medical professionals were on hand with their supplies ready to chip up to 2,000 individuals.

"Everyone, just follow the directions of my staff. They'll ensure no one leaves this facility un-chipped. Before I leave, how many of you know The Pledge?" Senator Johnson asked.

People in the crowd began to shout out the words of the pledge campaign. "I pledge allegiance to the chip and the safety, security, and convenience for which it stands, with one unified government, financial system, and religion for all."

Pastor McFarland was having a meeting on the steps of City Hall at the same time Senator Johnson was holding his meeting. He wanted to make the public aware of the plot that included a plan to control all living beings on Earth. He'd invited members of the press to hear what he had to say. Cho and his family were present, along with other church members, to show their support.

"There's a group out there, right now, down the street, promoting the implantable chip. It's my understanding they have medical professionals on hand to chip their attendees. Scripture in the Bible tells us to beware of antichrists."

Pastor McFarland opened his Bible, held it up, and said, "Read your Bibles. For it says in 1 John 2:18, 'Little children, it is the last hour; and as you have heard that the Antichrist is coming, even now many antichrists have come; by which we know that it is the last hour.' And in 1 John 2:22, 'Who is a liar but he who denies that Jesus is the Christ? He is antichrist who denies the Father and the Son.'"

Pastor McFarland looked sternly out into the crowd.

"There is not just one antichrist. There are many. They are antichrists in that they're presenting to you and promoting to you an antichrist system. A system whereby all will be required to have a character in his or her right hand or on his or her forehead to show their allegiance to a beastly system created to rule the world. The group out there now is focusing your attention on your right hand."

People in the crowd began to raise signs they'd been given and chanted, "I'm a believer. I'm a believer. I'm a believer of Jesus Christ and His Word!"

"What we're seeing is prophecy being revealed. On TV, radio, print and on social media, we're seeing more and more messages promoting the implantable chip. Its proponents started saying it was for identification purposes for the sick and elderly. That it would contain vital health information, say for instance, critical information for someone who became unconscious. But I assure you, there's a bigger agenda than you or I could ever conceive. And what you need to know is that the Bible talks about those who did not receive the mark — how they lived and reigned with Christ. Don't be deceived by their most recent messages of safety, security, and convenience."

People in the crowd raised other signs and started to chant, "No chip! No chip! No chip!"

Pastor McFarland continued, "I don't care how they spin it… the chip device and the system that will be used control it closely resemble what the Bible speaks of in reference to the beast and his mark. Again, a beastly system created to rule over all of mankind. Revelation thirteen, verse sixteen states, 'He causeth all, both small and great, rich and poor, free and slave, to receive a mark in their right hand or on their foreheads.'"

He reached into his suit pocket and pulled out a tiny object.

"This object symbolizes what the creators tout as the greatest advancement of mankind. Through the years, technology has been sanctioned as the advancements needed to make your life transactions easier. Probably most recognized is the technology that's impacted all generations; that is, the advancements in the way we communicate. For the old schoolers, from telephone landlines to smart phones and tablets; the ability not only to speak using one of these devices, but also to see who you're speaking to. From farm irrigation systems, medical treatment, to education teaching tools, and so much more; all in an effort to get you comfortable with this, the latest and greatest of technological advancements."

From the excitement of the crowd, Pastor McFarland sensed his message was sinking in.

"Warn your family members and friends to be careful what and who they listen to and follow on social media. The man who has spent the last decade of his life enhancing the functionality of radio frequency identification (RFID) technology to identify, track, and provide information on every living organism via an implantable chip goes by the name of Natas. If you spell his name in reverse, it would be Satan."

Someone in the crowd yelled out, "Oh my goodness!"

"God is the creator of all things that are of the Earth and on the Earth. Everything you see, He created. God gave man the knowledge and ability to make all the things he needed for existence on the Earth. Machines. Buildings. Technology. Food. Now man wants to take it upon himself to do what he wants and believes he has the knowledge and ability to do without God. For example, you have doctors and scientists thinking their ability to do great things and make great discoveries is due to their own knowledge and talent. Without God, man can't do anything. God is so gracious, and He lets us think it's us. He allows man to take credit for things. He is so gracious that He allows us to go day by day without worshipping Him, knowing He created us to praise and worship Him."

A man yelled, "Pastor Dobbs and his followers should be stoned to death, like they did in the biblical days!"

Pastor McFarland responded, "No, that's not the answer to what's happening now. We should all have kindness toward Pastor Dobbs and his followers and not be judgmental and unkind. It's true, he's blind to God's word. At this point, all we can do is love and pray for him and his followers. To have power, control, and money at the helm of one's thoughts and actions is a deadly weapon. But it's not our place to judge him or his followers, or anyone else. To do so would be hypocrisy on our part. God is the judge. I'll be praying for their salvation before it's too late. We've all been granted the right to choose. I'm praying they'll read the word of God and open their eyes to His will so they can choose God's route to their salvation. And I advise everyone here today to do the same. As it states in the Bible, it's not God's desire that anyone should perish, but many will, because they've elected to live the way they want, and not the way God desires for us to live for His Glory."

CHAPTER 7

The details for Ivan Shepherd's (Mo Money Monte) release from prison had been finalized. He was assigned a parole counselor, with whom he'd met, who then sent his mother a home plan a month before Ivan's visit with the parole board. His mother had consented to Ivan living with her, and she completed the required documents and sent them back to Ivan's parole counselor. Within days, a parole officer visited Ivan's mother to inspect her home. Ivan's hearing with the parole board ensued shortly thereafter. A week later, Ivan received notification that the parole board had released him on parole. He was transferred to the Walls Prison Unit in Huntsville, Texas, where he was picked up by his mother. To ensure compliance with his Release Certificate, he had to report to his parole officer within 24 hours.

Mo Money Monte's Release Certificate was reviewed by his parole officer, Mr. Elly Nelson, a beefy, heavyset man in his late forties who had been a parole officer for the Texas Department of Criminal Justice for nearly 20 years. Mr. Nelson met Mo Money Monte in the lobby and escorted him back to his office, where Mo Money Monte sat inches away from Mr. Nelson's desk.

"I'm not gonna read the rules and conditions to you again. If you give me a few good months, you'll be released from parole," he informed him. He proceed to discuss necessary referrals.

Nelson had a very intimidating look about him as he scribbled notes in Mo Money Monte's file. He looked at Mo Money Monte and grinned a sadistic grin.

"By the way, what name do you prefer? Ivan, or Mo Money Monte?"

"Ivan Shepherd."

"Anybody other than you would be referred to the Texas Workforce Commission for employment pursuits. Since your release was arranged for a specific purpose, there's no need for all of that."

"What do you mean for a specific purpose?"

Mr. Nelson proceeded while dismissing Mo Money Monte's inquiry. "Mr. Shepherd, I don't expect any trouble out of you. Just do what you were released to do, and everything will be favorable for you."

"What do you mean 'do what I was released to do'?"

"The fine details aren't for me to discuss. Just know your freedom from barred windows, rusted bars, metal toilets, hard cots, prison uniforms, and rats dashing through the cell blocks at Beeville comes with a price."

"Mr. Nelson, I was wrongly imprisoned. My release is the only favorable outcome to the years I've lost."

"All required fees are due monthly, via money order. With the amount you're about to make, I know that won't be a problem for you. Sign here."

Mr. Nelson pushed a pile of papers in front of Mo Money Monte, then went through and explained each piece of paper Mo Money Monte needed to sign.

"Any questions?"

Mo Money Monte didn't respond.

"Fine. Let me get you your copies." Mr. Nelson walked over to the copier in his office and began to make copies of the paperwork. "You'll need to obtain a Texas Department of Public Safety Driver's License or Identification Card." Placing the documents in a folder, Mr. Nelson stated, "And know that you'll need to extinguish your religious involvement with Pastor McFarland. Eyes will be on you from this day forward."

Mo Money Monte remained silent as he turned his head to look out Mr. Nelson's office window.

Mr. Nelson leaned back in his chair and said, "Non-compliance will land you back in jail or dead. Make no mistake about your future and your compliance. Your incarceration was intentional. Your stabbings while in prison were intentional. Your release was intentional. Your proper response must be intentional. I'll be contacting you within the next ten days to make a home visit and talk about your next office visit."

Mo Money Monte couldn't force his eyes away from the window.

There was a knock on Mr. Nelson's office door.

"Come in."

The door opened, and Larry Shepherd entered. Mr. Nelson closed a folder on his desk and walked out. Shocked, Mo Money Monte stood up.

Mo Money Monte stared petulantly at Larry. His eyes narrowing, he asked his biological father, "What are you doing here?"

"Son, I'm here to take you home."

"Take me home?! What are you talking about?"

"Wherever you need to go. You can stay with me and my wife until you get things situated."

"What are you talking about? Where is this coming from?"

"Son, I've made some big mistakes where you're concerned. I denied you. Never helped your mother financially to take care of you. Never visited you."

"Yes, you're right. And I definitely don't need you now!"

"I'm ashamed of how I treated you and your mom. All I want to do now is try and make things in your life right. When a person is young, all they see is what they need to do to provide for their family. I was married when your mother gave birth to you. I had so many dreams and aspirations. The disclosure of you would have meant disclosure of my infidelity. I thought it was best to keep you a secret."

"Right. A secret."

Larry's eyes began to water. He said, "I'm so sorry, son. My actions were inexcusable. But I'm here now, seeking your forgiveness. I know you know about forgiveness. I know you know the scripture Mark eleven, verse twenty-five — *And whenever you stand praying, if you have anything against anyone, forgive him, that your Father in heaven may also forgive you your trespasses.* And the scripture Matthew six, verse fifteen - *But if you do not forgive men their trespasses, neither will your Father forgive your trespasses.*"

"Why now?" Mo Money Monte commanded.

"After I learned about your incarceration and all that's happened to you, I realized it was my fault. Had I been involved in your life, I know things would have been different."

"I've been incarcerated for four years! You ignored my calls from prison for four years. As a matter of fact, you've ignored me all of my life."

"Son, I'm so sorry. Since your recent telephone call and letter, I've been working behind the scenes, working my connections to get you released."

"Working your connections?! Really?!"

"Yes. My plan to get you released had to be perfectly orchestrated."

"So, you're saying my release is because of you."

"Yes, son. That's the least I could do for you. But now I want to do more."

"More like what?"

"I want to help you get your life back on track. I want to help you continue the great work you were doing with your music."

"I don't need you for that."

"I know you don't, but I want to help you."

"Help me how?"

"My company, Global Media Sources, has joined the ranks to acquire and launch its own music streaming service. I've already arranged for you and Bone Esquire to be touted as artists who own their own music streaming service. I know they'd love having you and Bone Esquire on a unity tour, promoting the service. The promotional dollars have already been provided. The title everyone will be hash tagging will be #Alpha&Omega MafiaMyChipAccessforAll."

"No can do," Mo Money Monte said calmly. "My genre of music is now Gospel. I only rap for my Lord and Savior, Jesus Christ. And I have my own producers, MasterMark."

"Son, what I have for you will make you a global sensation."

"Not interested. Thank you for making your second visit to see me. It's odd that your visit is during my parole officer visit. I sent you several letters to your company, Global Media Sources, but you never responded back to me."

"Come on, son, let me help you," he pleaded.

Mo Money Monte looked around Mr. Nelson's office. He stared at a shelf stacked with criminology books and said abruptly, "Thank you for the scripture quotes. I didn't need you to recite them to me. I live by the scriptures Matthew eighteen, twenty-one through twenty-two — *Then Peter came to Him and said, 'Lord, how often shall my brother sin against me, and I forgive him? Up to seven times?' Jesus said to him, 'I do not say to you, up to seven times, but up to seventy times seven.'* I forgive you, Mr. Shepherd." He exited the office in a huff.

Larry walked quickly after him and yelled out, "Son. Wait a minute."

Mo Money Monte continued down a hallway.

Larry watched as Mo Money Monte embraced a young lady who was waiting for him in the lobby.

She noticed Larry watching them and asked, "Who's that man?"

Mo Money Monte responded abruptly, "My biological father, the secretive, deceitful Deacon Shepherd. Let's get out of here."

Through the multitude of people milling around in the office, Pamela Hobbs gave Larry Shepherd a look. He instantly smiled back at her.

Pam drove Mo Money Monte to his mother's home, where he would reside until he started earning some income. He and Pam walked in on his mother, Ms. Mascot, who was in the kitchen cutting fruit on her kitchen island. She was assembling the ingredients to make a smoothie for lunch. She'd been separating pieces of fresh cantaloupe, strawberries, and bananas.

"Hi, Mom," he said as they entered the kitchen.

"Hi, son," she responded. As he and his mother embraced, Mo Money Monte kissed her on the cheek. She looked over at Pam, who was wearing a tight-fitting dress, and said, "Thank you for taking Ivan to his first parole officer visit."

Pam smiled at Mo Money Monte and said, "You're welcome. No problem at all. I want to help Ivan in any way I can."

Pam had made it a point to monitor Mo Money Monte's prison stay through Pastor McFarland. After learning about his release and obtaining his contact information from Pastor McFarland, she reached out to him. Their meeting and connection during his stay in the hospital had intrigued her.

As Pam sat down at the kitchen table, Mo Money Monte excused himself to go use the restroom. Very tense, his mother started taking the fruit from the plastic containers and dropping pieces into her blender. She poured in a half cup of soy milk and orange juice, then waited to turn on the blender.

"My son said he met you during a hospital stay."

"Yes, ma'am. I was part of the team who helped him with his recovery from the stabbings."

"I see."

"You have a very talented son. While at the hospital, he shared some of his music with me. Very intriguing and thought-provoking."

"Yes, my son has always been very talented. But right now his focus should be on a fresh start," she insisted. "I don't know your intentions with my son, someone who was just released from prison and now on parole."

Pam interrupted Ms. Mascot, "I don't have any intentions, Ms. Mascot."

"I recently started to notice you during service at Triumphant Baptist Church. I must have been away the Sunday you united with the church," Ms. Mascot queried.

"I haven't officially united with the church. I started attending the early morning service after listening to Pastor McFarland on satellite radio. Ivan and I discovered we had the same church in common during his hospital stay. Since I'm part of Pastor McFarland's Life After Prison Reintegration Program, he paired Ivan with me to ensure access to the various programs that promote successful re-entry into society."

"Yes, I'm well aware of the program. I thought Pastor McFarland would be pairing Ivan with a male."

"Because of our connection, I did request Ivan," Pam admitted.

Ms. Mascot looked sternly and responded, "I don't bite my tongue when it comes to my son. Like I said earlier, I don't know your intentions, but I do know he doesn't need any distractions."

Looking puzzled, Pam said, "Are you thinking I'm a distraction for Ivan?"

Staring harshly at Pam, she declared, "His thoughts and actions must be focused on applying the lessons he's learned from past mistakes, and making sure he embraces a lifestyle and selects the right people to keep him on the right course."

Pam's smile faded as she listened to Ms. Mascot.

"Would you like a glass of water or orange juice? The orange juice is from fresh squeezed oranges. Or a cup of coffee? I only have enough fruit to make me a smoothie."

"I'll take a glass of orange juice."

She poured orange juice as Mo Money Monte walked in and sat down at the table next to Pam.

"Mom, guess who was at the parole office to see me?"

"Who?"

"My biological father."

"Larry Shepherd?" she said as she handed Pam the glass of orange juice.

"Yes!"

"What on Earth was he doing there?"

"Says he wants to make things up to me. Says Global Media can help me. Talked about making big mistakes and ignoring me all these years. Says Global Media has its own music streaming service and he's arranged for me and Bone Esquire to be touted as artists who own their own music streaming service. Something about a unity tour."

"Did you tell him you're only doing Gospel now?"

"Yes, I did."

"Son, I've never wanted to say anything negative to you about your father, but he's a liar. A deceitful man."

Pam sat intently listening to their back and forth conversation.

"Yes, Mother, I know. Go ahead and blend your fruit."

"Would you like a glass?"

"Sure."

Pam sat at the table, looking as though her efforts to win over his mother would be challenging. She thought, *She said she only had enough for one smoothie.*

Avoiding Pam's face, Ms. Mascot turned on the blender. When she finished, she retrieved two glasses from her cabinet, then started to pour the smoothie mixture into both.

"This tastes great," Mo Money Monte said as he drank the smoothie. "Mother, you don't have enough for Pam?"

Pam quickly interrupted and said, "I'm good, Ivan."

"Son, we need to get to the driver's license place so you can get your license," Ms. Mascot said.

"Okay."

"I can take you," Pam interjected.

"Thank you, Pam, but we have some other business to take care of," Ms. Mascot said with urgency.

"Thanks, Pam, for everything," Mo Money Monte said.

Pam smiled and gave him a hug, then turned and headed for the front door. Ms. Mascot's face was plainly strained. As Mo Money Monte walked Pam outside to her car, Ms. Mascot listened attentively at the front door.

"I'll look forward to seeing you tomorrow. Thank you, again, for taking me to my parole visit."

Ms. Mascot's ability to hear the remainder of their conversation was diminished when Pam sat inside her car.

Ms. Mascot waited impatiently for Mo Money Monte to return inside. As she started moving boxes of outdated papers that lingered in the hallway, Mo Money Monte walked back inside.

"Mother, let me get those boxes for you. Where do you want them?"

"In the garage for now is fine."

"Okay."

Mo Money Monte proceeded to move ten small boxes into the garage.

"Mother, what do you have in these boxes?" he asked.

Ms. Mascot followed him in and out as he carried the boxes.

"Just old financial papers. Papers I should have gotten rid of. Let's go, so we can stop by the church."

"Yes, Pastor McFarland wants to see me. There are a lot of things going on, and he's assembling a platform to warn folks."

"Warn people about the chip?" she asked.

"Yes, ma'am. Plus, I need to let him know about my dad's visit at the parole office."

Ms. Mascot grabbed her purse off the kitchen countertop, and they left.

On their twenty-minute drive to Triumphant Baptist Church, Mo Money Monte received a text message from Bone Esquire. It read, "Hey Mo! Need to meet with you ASAP. Got something going on. BIG! Lots of money! Call me!!!"

Ms. Mascot noticed the troubled look on Mo Money Monte's face.

"What are you reading?" his mother asked.

"It's a text message from Bone."

"What does he want?"

"Talking about something BIG."

"Ignore it."

"Doing so."

A heavy drizzle began falling as they were driving. Mo Money Monte gazed at the street names from Interstate 30 as they made their way to the church, which was located in Garland, TX. South Haskell Ave., East Grand Ave., Military Pkwy., and N. Buckner Blvd. He was excited about the opportunity to be directly involved with Pastor McFarland's Vision 2030 Campaign. The rain started to fall harder.

Mo Money Monte thought about Pam and said, "Mother, you were sort of cold to Pam."

"Yeah, I know…Ivan."

"Mother, she was so nice to me when I ended up in the hospital. She's tracked my prison stay and release. She really likes me."

"She appears to like you, son."

"What do you mean, appears to…?"

"There's something about her. I can't put my finger on it, but something about her isn't right. Trust a mother's instinct, son."

"She knows all about my music—since my very beginning. Now that I've switched, she's supportive of me and my Gospel music. She's very pretty, smart, and a nurse. Nurses are good people. She's been a part of medical personnel in Iraq, caring for our wounded soldiers. Above all, she's involved in Pastor McFarland's Life After Prison Reintegration Program. She's so much different than the women I've been connected to in the past."

"I'm sure, son. Just tread slowly with her."

"Okay, Mother."

"Find out as much as you can about her. Use that Internet. You can find out anything about anybody. Verify where she's told you she's from. Who are her people? I'm assuming she's not married. Has she ever been married? Kids? How long has she been a nurse? Who has she worked for? What schools did she attend? Are her parents alive? If so, where do they live? Does she have siblings? If so, where do they live? Other relatives? Cousins? Who does she associate with? Does she drink or smoke? Drugs? They tell me social media will tell you a lot about a person."

Mo Money Monte and his mother, who was the church secretary, entered the church building. Pastor McFarland appeared, walking down the hallway, looking red-eyed and fatigued.

"Hi, Pastor," Mo Money Monte said.

Pastor McFarland proceeded to greet Mo Money Monte and his mother. He gave Ms. Mascot a kiss on her forehead.

Mo Money Monte shook his hand and said, "You okay, Pastor?"

"Just a lot of corruption going on. Inside information I'm being given, along with what we're seeing is prophesy at work."

"I'll be in the office while you visit with Pastor. I need to work on Sunday's program and some other materials Pastor would like distributed on Sunday."

"Okay, Mother."

Pastor McFarland invited Mo Money Monte to walk with him to his office.

"I'm so glad everything worked out for you and that you were released from prison."

"Thank you, Pastor. I'm not sure, but I'm thinking it was all planned."

"Why do you think that?"

"My father showed up out of the blue at my parole visit."

"Really?"

"Yes, really. I don't know if you know the story about me, my mother, and my father."

"Yes, I do. Your mother recently shared it with me. She always hoped you'd unite with a church. All the while I knew you in prison, I wasn't aware she was your mother."

"She never approved of the lifestyle my music attracted."

"And rightfully so."

"I'll assure you that my father's appearance is no coincidence."

"Samuel Cho, one of our members, will be here shortly. He works for Global Media Sources. He's been sharing some of the goings on at the company. There's something big in the works. Also, Senator Ryan Paul Patrick will be here shortly."

"What are you thinking?"

"I'm thinking we need to get a hard and heavy message out. Their pledge campaign is having a huge impact."

"Yes. It's popping up all over the place. 'I pledge allegiance to the chip and the safety, security, and convenience for which it stands, with one unified government, financial system, and religion for all.'"

"Organizers have been working behind the scenes on the New World Access for years, and now it's becoming increasingly more visible. They're becoming bold and coming out of the closet. There's a new group of militants with worldwide impact, the SAVERS, that's emerged. I know they're connected to the grand scheme of the implantable chip."

"What does the acronym SAVERS stand for?"

"Shared Access Victors Elect Responsible System."

"Oh my!"

Mo Money Monte's cell telephone was vibrating as Pastor McFarland was talking. It was Pam, texting him.

"Is someone trying to reach you?" Pastor McFarland asked.

"It's Pam Hobbs."

"Well, answer if you believe it's important."

"I'm good. I'll respond after our meeting. Mother believes something is off about her."

"She recently started visiting here. She hasn't officially joined. Some folks like to date us for a while before they commit."

They both laughed.

"She's helped out tremendously with the ministry program. On her off days, she volunteers to help our women with job search, medical resources, and government resources. She came in and really got to work with enhancing our programs. I'm hopeful she'll unite with us."

Minutes later, both Cho and Senator Ryan Paul Patrick arrived.

"Have a seat, gentlemen," Pastor McFarland said, pointing to empty chairs in front of his desk. "I'm glad you were able to meet with me today."

Pastor McFarland took time to introduce and familiarize the gentlemen with Mo Money Monte.

"Ivan helped me do some wonderful things inside the prison while he was incarcerated. Ivan and I were talking earlier about the Pledge campaign currently being circulated. Cho, can you share with the gentlemen other things you're aware of?"

"Well, I'm not being invited to many of the company discussions, but I know Global Media Sources has entered into agreements with numerous service and business entities to provide free reader equipment and the My Access Chip software technology. The initiative was designed for companies to improve and foster next generation services and products. All they need to do is include in the promotional and marketing materials a message to encourage their users and customers to download their app, share, and get a free My Access Chip. The tag will be 'Convenience. Connection. Comfort.'"

"The other day, I received a telephone call from Betty Shepherd. She said her husband is Larry Shepherd with Global Media Sources. Do you know him, Cho?"

"Yes, he's my counterpart. And he's heavily involved in all that's happening. Definitely spearheading a large majority of it."

"She said he beats her and is forcing her and their children to get chipped. She's afraid for her life."

"Are we going to help her?" Cho asked.

"Absolutely. The Underground is working to get her, the kids, and her mother to a safe house."

"Great!" Cho responded.

"She'll be in a safe place very soon."

"Let me know if they need any help. I know Larry is a by-any-means necessary person. I have no doubt he'll employ extreme measures if she doesn't comply," Cho assured them.

"We know. She's been advised to hang in there until we can get everything finalized regarding their movement."

Pastor McFarland was known worldwide for speaking out and taking action against domestic violence. He had instituted a domestic violence program that offered information and training for impacted families. A part of the program that wasn't publicized was the Underground Promise Land. It was the part of their offerings that provided shelter to those whose lives were in danger. Pastor McFarland had a network of secret safe houses established throughout the United States. Women and children needing an escape from danger were taken off in the middle of the night to one of the underground safe houses. Only a handful of people were aware of the Underground Promise

Land. Women and children on the move would eventually be given a new identity—a new life.

"Ivan, we need you to get out there to reach the younger audience. You have a name that needs rebranding, rebranding in the context that your followers know you're working for the kingdom. You have the one song, *Awakened to His Presence*."

"I've been working on one that addresses the chip. Listen," he said as he began to rap. "Don't be deceived by the rhetoric behind the chip. To say it'll enhance your convenience and comfort is a trick. Make no mistake, it's strictly focused on creating chaos to facilitate control. Pay attention to the random acts of violence and terror trying to influence your soul. These acts are perfectly orchestrated as an agent of panic and persuasion to fuel their vested mission. So you'll see no alternative but to get chipped and maximize their vision," Mo Money Monte finished with a smile.

"It's a great start," Senator Ryan acknowledged.

Back at the Global Media Sources TV Station, news anchor Jenny Purdue was preparing to air a breaking news story. The TV cameras zoomed in on her. There was an image of the nation's capital behind her.

"Today on Nation's Access, we're beginning in high alert about the SAVERS. Just back from London, let's go to our news correspondent, Michael O'Donald."

Michael O'Donald started his account of what was happening. "With continued attacks in Iraq and Syria, the SAVERS group is on the move, making its presence known throughout the United States and Canada. With the recent terror attacks in Midland, Texas, Santa Barbara, California, and London, their recruitment efforts in the U.S. and Europe are seemingly unstoppable. Our government's response to them is paralyzing."

"What is the United States' answer for resolving a crisis concern?"

"The United States is activating its options for containing the SAVERS' attacks overseas. Up to now, in comparison to another militant group a few years ago, the SAVERS have been successful with seizing the borders of Ramadi, Baghdad and other prominent areas."

Jenny Purdue interrupted, "Let's go to foreign correspondent Miles Windfall, who's just returned from Baghdad. He joins us from Paris."

Miles talked about the SAVERS gaining control by taking cities, and the blood bath the SAVERS fighters had underway.

Jenny Purdue asked, "And the U.S.' strategy for handling the SAVERS. We have Mark McPhaul and Timothy Slater on the intelligence platform waiting via satellite to talk about solutions for stopping the SAVERS and their recruits through social media."

Mark McPhaul started off with, "First, we're encouraging all to get chipped. The chip is our way of ensuring safety and security for everyone."

"Is our security at risk?" Jenny asked.

"Yes, it is. Overseas, people are being executed and left on the streets. The SAVERS' movement is now acting in full force throughout the U.S. I guarantee you'll start to see more and more bloodshed."

"What about our troops?" Jenny inquired further.

"With the growing surge of the SAVERS, we won't have enough troops to protect us."

"Timothy, give us your perspective."

"Political battles, lack of military support…that's what we're facing," Timothy Slater said.

"What can we do as Americans?"

"The massacre in Midland, the deliberate train crash by the conductor in Vancouver, the incitement of racial attacks by police departments, and on and on and on. The actions are the works of the SAVERS and their recruitment of assassins. Those who are being touted as the Modern Day Saviors. Getting chipped is our surveillance tool."

Bone Esquire was minutes away from kicking off the first of a series of concerts. His limo turned onto McKinney Ave in Dallas, TX, and there it was, The New Access Club, only three yards ahead. A throng of fans was spilling out of the club, off the sidewalk, and into the street. Bone Esquire and Spiderman stared ahead in amazement.

"Just think if Mo Money Monte was here with us," Spiderman said.

"No need to think about him right now. He's not here and may never want to be here with us."

"That'll be unfortunate."

"Yes, it'll definitely be unfortunate for him and his family. We're hoping his father's insider will be the key to him changing his mind."

The sound of the fans could be heard as they pulled up to the entrance. As the fans realized who was inside, they began to react by chanting the words, "Bone! Bone! We love you, Bone!"

"This is crazy!" Bone shouted.

"This is what you've been trying to get back to," Spiderman said.

As Bone and Spiderman exited the limo, there was a parade of My Access TV cameras, lights, photographers, and fans adorning the red carpet. Four security guards positioned themselves to hold back the fans.

Mr. Mole stepped out of nowhere, wearing a tuxedo, and said to Bone, "Take some pictures, then they're taking you straight back to the Alpha&Omega Room."

Bone nodded his head.

"Get ready to render a jaw-dropping, magical concert," Spiderman said as they walked the red carpet.

"Right!"

Bone looked out into a haziness of hands and faces. Energized fans. A crowd chanting "Bone Esquire! Bone Esquire! Bone Esquire!"

Bone raised his hand and started to speak. "It's captivating headlines all over the world. Controversy. The opposition says you're being enticed to boldly step into uncharted territory. I say they're a lie!"

Bone was submerged in light and the round of applause from the huge audience.

"I say unprecedented access is what you'll experience."

Bone started to rap his new song, *Unprecedented Access*.

"Take a look at my hand that houses a unique device. No doubt, it's sophisticated and powerful, resembling a small grain of rice. You too can have it implanted inside. This medical-grade glass casing that stores and transmits data for all of mankind. If unprecedented access to a new world of super-sized luxurious lifestyle is what you desire. I guarantee you this implantable chip will be a worthy companion to access networks that will help the mobility of your transactions thrive. Its opposition says it's about control. A form of manipulation. I'm here to tell you it's a straight up upgrade designed to facilitate your own one-stop-shop secure access panel."

The crowd started chanting, "Bone Esquire! Bone Esquire! Bone Esquire! #Alpha&OmegaMafiaMyChipAccessforAll!"

CHAPTER 8

It was an unusually warm spring Sunday in Dallas, TX. Planned activities were on the horizon to weed out non-supporters and get more and more people chipped. Samuel Cho was across town in old Grand Prairie, TX, standing in the parking lot where his business had burned down.

"Hi, Mr. Cho," Stanley said loudly as he approached him on his bike. "You're usually at church about this time, right?"

Stanley was the son of the janitor who had cleaned Cho's buildings for nearly twenty years.

"Hi, Stanley," Cho responded. "Where are you coming from, son?"

Stanley got off his bike and answered, "Just riding through the neighborhood, trying to figure out what I'm gonna do next. I'll be graduating in May."

"Wow! That's so wonderful," Cho said with excitement.

"I'll be sure to send you an invitation."

"Wonderful. I'll look forward to attending. Which college have you decided on?"

Stanley looked perplexed, not sure what to say, knowing his plans to attend college had changed.

"You are going to college, right?" Cho questioned.

"No, sir," Stanley said, holding onto his bike.

Looking confused, Cho said, "I have a specific memory of a conversation your father and I had when you were a young boy."

"What was it?"

Cho smiled and recounted, "He knew you would make a great reporter someday. He often talked about your love for reading and writing. He even shared a couple of your short story writings with me, which I found to be really good. He talked about how you wrote for your high school's newspaper and how you were good at listening, getting the details, and describing the facts."

Stanley stood engrossed in what Cho was saying, sadly pondering his words.

"So, it saddens me to hear you aren't pursuing college," Cho said sympathetically.

"The money just isn't there, Mr. Cho."

"I know he was placing money into a college fund for you," Cho said.

Stanley started to twist the front of his bike and said, "I know my parents started it."

"So what happened?"

"I really don't know."

Cho sensed he wasn't going to get answers to the questions he was seeking, so he decided to go about getting clarity a different way.

"How's your mother doing?" Cho asked.

"She's doing okay, sir."

"I've been meaning to come by and check on you all. Between work and my daughter's care, I've been so consumed."

Glad the subject had changed, Stanley asked, "How's Adrika?"

"She's adjusting to her new life," Cho acknowledged. "It's been a long journey. Many surgeries, but she's been a soldier through them all. She never complained once."

Stanley responded, "I still remember us at the junior prom. She was so beautiful. Being much younger, I was so proud to accompany her."

Cho's head dropped in sadness.

"I'm so sorry, Mr. Cho. I didn't mean to say…"

Cho interrupted Stanley abruptly, "It's okay."

"Life has been difficult all around. Dad's death has been so overwhelming for my mom."

"I know it was."

"She's having a really tough time."

"Tough time?" Cho repeated with concern.

"Yes, emotionally and financially. Whatever money there may have been in a college fund, I'm pretty sure it went towards the medical bills for my father. Between his stroke and brain cancer, the medical bills depleted their savings. More so than anything, the quality of the health care my dad received once we lost our health insurance was crazy."

"That is so unfortunate," Cho responded.

"I sure hate that health care reform wasn't in place. The hospital, basically, sent him home to die. All they were worried about was inserting a chip in him."

"Your dad had a chip?" Cho inquired.

"Yes. The doctors said it was necessary if something happened to him."

Cho stood emotionless.

"Now I have it," Stanley announced.

"You have it?" Cho shouted.

"Yes! Even though it's a pilot program at Manning High School. Don't you have the chip?" Stanley inquired as he raised his hand. "They told my mom that all students needed it for safety purposes. I even wrote a piece about it for our newspaper. I interviewed students, teachers, counselors, and parents. Parents really like it. They like having the ability to track the movements of their kids."

Cho eyed Stanley's hand.

Stanley was so happy about his implantable chip. "I was okay with it once I saw all the entertainers getting them, like the rapper Bone Esquire."

Cho remained silent, fighting to stay calm.

"Well, I better get home. I hope to see you again soon. I'm turning nineteen next month. Do you think you could help me get on with your company? Maybe I could get on as a reporter."

Hesitating as he spoke, Cho responded, "I'll check with our human resources department to find out if there are some intern positions. We need to focus on getting you enrolled in college."

"Yes, I'd love to work in the department, reporting the plane crashes, hotel bombings, missing people..."

"I'll have to see what's available."

"Thank you so much, Mr. Cho. I'll look forward to hearing from you. I'd better be getting home. My mom is probably getting worried about me."

Stanley hopped on his bike and rode off.

After graduation, Stanley made a visit to Cho's company. When he mentioned Samuel Cho to the receptionist, she immediately referred him to Larry Shepherd.

"Hi, Mr. Shepherd," Stanley said.

"Hi, Stanley. I hear you're here to see Samuel Cho."

"Yes, sir!" Stanley said with excitement. "I mentioned to him recently that I was interested in working for Global Media Sources. He said he'd check with your human resources department, but I haven't from him. I know he's a busy man, so I'm just here today to follow up with him."

"How do you know Cho?"

"My father worked as his janitor for over twenty years."

"I see."

Larry stared for a moment at Stanley, thinking he'd be a great fit for their social media initiative.

"I like a young man who knows how to follow up," Larry smiled.

"Yes, sir!"

"What's your last name?"

"James, Stanley James."

"Since Cho isn't available, I'll be happy to visit with you. Tell me about your background, Stanley James."

"The only experience I have is writing for my school's newspaper. I brought some of my writings."

Stanley handed Larry a manila folder. Larry started flickering through the papers. He noticed an article entitled, *Glory to the Chip*.

"What is this article about?"

"It's about the implantable chip."

Larry started to view the contents of the article. He began to read a section of the article aloud, "Negative perspectives can sway and cause doubt, but I assure you the glory of the My Access Chip in a complicated and uncertain world is our only saving device. So what if our parents can track our every movement? I'd rather my mother have the capability to find me if I'm taken by the SAVERS group. Am I excited about having the chip implanted inside of me? Yes, but just like all of you, I'm conflicted, too. But when I think about the world we're living in, it's more important for me to have the chip as my protection shield. "

"You like those words, Mr. Shepherd?"

"I sure do, Stanley."

"Mr. Cho said he knew I was good at listening, getting the details, and describing the facts. My intentions are to go to college, but because of the financial hardships my family is experiencing right now, I need to work."

"Well, today is your lucky day, Stanley, if you're interested in an opportunity we currently have available."

"Sir, I already know I'm interested. What is it?"

"Because of your article, it sounds like you have the chip."

"Yes, sir, I sure do."

"Wonderful. We're looking for someone who loves posting on social media," Larry said as he handed Stanley's folder back to him.

"Sir, I post all day. Throughout the day," Stanley said with excitement.

"Global Media Sources has accepted a huge project to create increased awareness and visibility about getting chipped. We're looking for someone who can rev up our current social media forums and create others. We need someone young like you, an 'Engager' who can head up a team promoting the chip. Even work with the IT team on developing apps and games."

"I can do it, sir! I practically live on the Internet."

"We need constant communications and interactions on any and all social media forums that inform, educate, and foster support of getting chipped."

"I can do it, sir!"

"Great! I need you to report here in the morning at seven o'clock."

"I'll be here at 6:30 a.m."

"Seven o'clock is fine. Our human resources department is on the sixth floor. You'll need to report there first to complete new hire paperwork. Then you'll come here afterwards. I'll introduce you to our Director of Public Relations, Melissa Waters."

From a distance down the hallway, Cho saw Stanley talking to Larry. Cho started to walk anxiously down the hallway towards Stanley and Larry. Curious about why Stanley was there and what they could be discussing, he was visibly preoccupied with concern. Cho saw the noticeably excited Stanley headed for the elevator. Larry had just finished explaining to Stanley the full scope of his responsibilities. Stopping short of reaching them, Cho yelled out to Stanley.

Turning around, Stanley smiled and said, "Hi, Mr. Cho!"

"Hold up," Cho said as he walked quickly towards Stanley.

Cho rushed by Larry and asked, "Stanley, what are you doing here?"

"I came looking for you."

"Did you need something? Is your mother okay?"

"Yes, sir. All is well," Stanley assured him. "I came to inquire about the job I asked you about."

"What job?"

"The job I asked you to check on. To see what Global may have had available."

Cho started to remember their conversation the last time they spoke.

"I'm so sorry, I completely forgot."

"It's okay. I know you're busy. That's why I stopped by."

Larry was still standing nearby in a corner, listening to their discussion.

"No worries. Mr. Shepherd has offered me a job here," Stanley said in an ecstatic tone.

Cho had a reaction of surprise.

Larry approached them and said, "Yes, Cho, Stanley will be working with Melissa Waters to manage all our social media tools for the new project."

Cho had a confused look. "He doesn't have that sort of experience."

"He doesn't have to have experience. He'll be posting and monitoring feedback for us."

Stanley interrupted respectfully, "I know all about social media, Mr. Cho. I promise I'll do a good job. I'll make you so proud of me."

"We know you will, Stanley," Larry said calmly. "We'll see you in the morning."

"Thank you again! I can't wait to tell my mother," Stanley said as he quickly walked away.

Cho looked at Larry and said, "He doesn't belong here."

"What are you talking about?"

"You just want to manipulate him into doing your dirty work."

"You're right, Cho. I want to manipulate his amazing social media talents."

Cho looked at Larry with contempt.

"You're making it real tough on yourself, Cho."

"What are you talking about?"

"All I'll say is, one day real soon."

Cho knew Larry's comments were an attempt to instigate a negative reaction, so he simply retreated and walked away.

The following day, Stanley reported for work as instructed. While he was completing paperwork in the human resources office, Cho walked in, looking for Stanley. He noticed the receptionist at her desk looking at some papers. Stanley was sitting in a corner at a cubicle with his head down.

Cho walked over to Stanley and said, "I don't think this is a good move for you, Stanley."

Startled by his sudden appearance, Stanley responded, "Hi, Mr. Cho." He was confused by his statement.

The receptionist overheard Cho's comment to Stanley and started to listen intensely.

"Huh? What are you talking about, Mr. Cho?"

"There's a reason I didn't refer you to my company."

"Why, Mr. Cho? You know I needed a job. That my mother is relying on me to help out financially."

"This is a very corrupted environment. Your father was like a brother to me, and I don't want his son getting caught up in the things they're doing around here."

"What things, Mr. Cho?"

"The chip!"

"What about the chip?"

"The conspiracy to make it mandatory."

"The chip is cool, Mr. Cho. I'm okay with it. I'm glad I got it for free at my high school."

"The chip is not cool, Stanley! There's a higher plan no one knows about."

"What plan is that?"

"The plan that will enable one system to control everyone with the chip! You won't be able to make a move, buy or purchase goods and services, travel to another city, or use the restroom without this system tracking your every move."

The receptionist kept her head down and her ears turned towards Cho and Stanley. As they continued to talk, she sent an email to Mr. Meyers' secretary so she could make him aware of the conversation taking place.

Moments later, Mr. Meyers walked into the human resources office. Cho and Stanley's conversation was interrupted by Mr. Meyers' presence. The three men exchanged weak glances, then Mr. Meyers looked specifically at Cho for a moment before speaking.

He turned towards Stanley and said, "Hi, Stanley. I'm Matt Meyers, President of Global Media Sources. Larry Shepherd told me about you yesterday. We're very excited to have you on the team. How's it going so far?"

Stanley stood up to shake his hand.

"It's good, Mr. Meyers. I got here a little early to get my paperwork completed."

"Great. When you get finished, report to Larry Shepherd's office so he can get you started with Melissa Waters, our Director of Public Relations. She and her team just finished creating the Whereaboutsaccess app. It'll be one of the first action items you'll start promoting on social media."

"I'm so excited. Will do, sir!"

Mr. Meyers gestured towards Cho and said, "Cho, I need to see you in my office."

The two men traded an uneasy glance and started to walk past the receptionist.

Stanley shouted out, "I'll see you later, Mr. Cho!"

Cho turned back and looked at him with a half-smile. As Mr. Meyers and Cho started out the door to the corridor, they passed Larry, who was on his way in to check on Stanley.

Larry was accompanied by Melissa Waters.

Cho sat in front of Mr. Meyers' desk. With a grim, piercing glance at Cho, Mr. Meyers began to speak as he walked around his desk.

"I would offer you something to drink, but you won't be here that long."

Cho sat still and uncomfortable in the chair.

"Do you have any idea what you've done?"

Cho looked at Meyers, frowned, and shrugged his shoulder.

"When we brought you onboard, we considered you one of our most valuable assets. We'd worked with you for many years through your business and knew your talent was what we needed to move our initiatives forward. We've tried to help you understand Project My Access Chip and the movement. Your suspicions. Your mistrust. Your judgment of this company and iTrack, Inc. Now insiders are telling us about your connection to Pastor McFarland, and how you're speaking out against us and the chip."

Cho sat unremorseful as he listened to Mr. Meyers.

Mr. Meyers snapped his finger and yelled out, "Are you crazy? The project we've commenced is very complex and needs committed contributors in place to ensure its success. Your commitment has been nonexistent for a while. We've come to realize your support and loyalty aren't where we need them. More importantly, we've determined your presence at Global Media Sources is no longer needed. And even more importantly, the consequences for jeopardizing our project will be severe."

Looking out the window thoughtfully, Cho asked, "So, are you firing me? Or are you threatening me?."

"Today will be your last day as an employee of Global Media Sources."

Deciding to add some humor to Mr. Meyers' announcement of his last working day, Cho responded, "Okay. I just want to be clear on why my employment is ending? I've received nothing but good reviews. No verbal or written warnings. No disciplinary actions due to insubordination, policy violations, gross misconduct, so I'm just wondering."

A stern-faced Meyers looked at Cho and said, "Just know your services are no longer needed in this organization. If you need a reason, then use this one: we've decided to eliminate your position due to budget cuts. Your duties will be combined with other positions in the organization."

"I'm assuming Larry Shepherd will inherit my job responsibilities?"

"You'll need to go by human resources to complete your exit paperwork."

"So abrupt," Cho said calmly. "Guess I was getting too close to finding out Global Media's real secrets."

"You'll get a month's severance pay, and a good reference."

"I'm a little confused. A good reference?"

"Yes. When you were good, you were good."

Understandably unresponsive, Cho stood and began walking out of Mr. Meyers' office — right into two men who appeared and stood at the entrance of Meyers' office door.

Stanley quickly started out impressing his bosses, and within weeks he'd become a social media sensation for Global Media Sources.

On a spur-of-the-moment visit to Dallas, TX, Jim Natas stopped by the Global Media Sources headquarters.

"What brings you to Dallas?" Mr. Meyers inquired.

"I flew in for a lunch date."

Smiling, Mr. Meyers said, "Must have been a pretty important lunch date."

"Yes, she was."

"While you're here, I'd love for you to meet our social media guru."

"Wonderful."

Mr. Meyers called his secretary and instructed her to have Stanley come to his office.

"We're a little over 2 million implants from our goal," Mr. Meyers shared. "Even with the opposition, we're hitting our targets."

"Now that's great news."

Stanley stuck his head in Mr. Meyers' office and said, "You wanted to see me, sir?"

"Yes, come in. I want you to meet Jim Natas, the owner of iTrack, Inc. and the creator of The My Access Chip."

"Wow!"

"It's nice to meet you, Stanley. I've been hearing about all the great things you're doing with social media to advance the movement."

Stanley moved quickly to shake Jim Natas' hand.

"His obsession with social media has definitely worked in our favor," Mr. Meyers stated. "Tell Mr. Natas about the 'Be SMART' campaign."

"Be SMART stands for 'Be safe minded against recurring terrorism,'" Stanley said. "It's another message to engage and communicate a recurring theme to be smart against what's looming."

"The attacks of the SAVERS," Natas commented.

"Absolutely. A caption underneath the message states, 'Your future can be safer than it was yesterday without the chip.'"

"Our opposition has seen our message and counteracted with their own Be SMART campaign."

"What does theirs stand for?" Natas asked.

"Be spiritually mature absorbing redemptive truths," Stanley replied.

"Thank you, Stanley, for stopping by," Natas said.

"Thank you, sir. We also have the Whereaboutsaccess message finished for the app. It's simply a message about knowing the whereabouts of your loved ones and friends through your My Access Chip."

"Wonderful. Keep up the good work, Stanley."

"Will do, sir."

Stanley left the room.

"What is he doing to provoke interest in joining the SAVERS?" Mr. Natas inquired.

Stanley wasn't aware that the SAVERS were created by the Organizers. The Organizers knew they needed a new model of militants, and they wanted the SAVERS to be representative of American-born young people wreaking havoc throughout America. Melissa Waters had directed Stanley to foster social media activity on two different platforms for the My Access Chip. One platform would be fear driven. The other platform would be recruitment driven.

"Let me give you an example of what he's doing," Mr. Meyers said, beaming with enthusiasm.

Natas looked curiously at Mr. Meyers.

"My daughter, Chasity, has 3,000 friends on her iAccessBook page. It's taken a great deal of time, but so far Stanley has created 5,000 fake iAccessBook public pages. And he's connected them in an obscure way to her 3,000 friends."

"How so?"

"Okay, it's complicated, but let me try and explain. This social media stuff is new for me," Mr. Meyers laughed. "The 5,000 fake iAccessBook public pages depict people who are doing great things in the community, successful business owners, people who post inspirational messages that speak to one's thoughts and feelings, and people who post non-inspirational messages that speak to one's thoughts and feelings. These fake pages represent people from all walks of life. With these fake pages, he's becoming friends with like-minded people. Then through some backdoor way, he's able to create the appearance that my daughter's friends are becoming friends with other friends they have in common. The theory is, if I see we have friends in common, I'm more likely to become your friend as well."

"Interesting."

"Using the platform focused on fear, these like-minded people are posting all day about the chip. That is, posting about why it's critical to get chipped, the benefits of the chip, the protection it provides against the SAVERS, the messages included with the Be SMART campaign, and the free programs associated with the chip. Once again, if you see like-minded people getting chipped, you're more likely to get chipped. For example, if you see a runner getting chipped for safety reasons, you as a runner are more likely to be inspired to get chipped."

"How is he able to post about all those things throughout the day?"

"System programming. Melissa's team has programmed all the accounts. The same message may be posting to 1,000 of the fake pages simultaneously. I forgot to mention the pages of Representative Tadd Smith, Senator Johnson, Bone Esquire, Pastor Dobbs, and many others include daily postings about the chip."

"What about the recruitment platform?"

"Other fake pages have postings inviting people to be a part of something special. Messages like, 'You were created for a mission', 'Are you being held captive? We have a way to help you break free', 'It's time to make your mark on the world. Let us show you how'. Literally thousands of messages and images have been created for our recruitment purposes."

"What sort of images?"

"Images of men and women dressed in camouflage apparel with their weapons; an image that influences others to join those who are fighting for a cause."

"Whatever he's doing, it's working."

"Absolutely."

"Sorry about the impromptu visit. I just wanted to stop by before I head back to Louisiana."

"It was good to see you."

"I'll be looking forward to seeing even greater results of all you're doing and have in the works to do," Mr. Natas said with a smile.

He then shook Mr. Meyers' hand and walked out of his office.

CHAPTER 9

Monday, June 21, 2021, the beginning of summer, and the stage for increased planned catastrophes had been set. Reports of incidents were pouring into the news station from all over the world.

"Good evening, ladies and gentlemen. This is Jenny Purdue with My TrueAccess News."

"And I'm Martin Matthews with My TrueAccess World News."

"We bring you this special television broadcast to give you the latest information about events that are happening all over the world," Jenny Purdue said.

"Government and Defense Department officials are concerned by reports of panic in several small and large cities throughout the U.S. and overseas," Martin said. "Let's go to Lonnie Walker, who's in New York City near Central Park. Lonnie what's going on there?"

While panting, Lonnie started to speak into his microphone. On a building behind him was a clock that displayed 8:30 p.m. A foreign man ran up to him with excitement and panic, babbling into the news reporter's face about bombs placed underneath piles of trash on the streets of New York City. The news reporter started to make sense of what the man was saying and translated it from his native tongue. Bombs that had been strategically placed throughout New York City, in trash left on the streets for pickup, had exploded. Different cameras zoomed in on piles of trash on fire on 72nd Street, 34th Street, and 8th Avenue. It was reported that hundreds of people had been injured and taken to nearby hospitals.

Between the news breaks were commercials about the chip. "Chances are, you know someone who needs to get chipped. Maybe it's a family member, a friend, a colleague, or a neighbor. It's as easy as 1-2-3. Tell everyone you know to visit www.myaccesschip.com to find their nearest chipping location. We're counting on people like you to help us spread the word. Knowing you've already gotten chipped will mean a lot to those in your circle, and it means a lot to us to know there are folks like you out there doing your part to help others have peace of mind."

Jenny Purdue abruptly announced, "We have another report coming in from our reporter, Karan Khan." Karan Khan had started to report on a train crash and derailment in northern India. "Karan Khan is reporting that a passenger train has collided with a freight train. There are fifty fatalities and over 200 injured."

There was report after report after report. "A motorcyclist seen reeling in and out of traffic on George Washington Bridge, which runs between New Jersey and New York City, has exploded. Cars alongside him that were traveling to their various destinations were hit with burning debris. Suddenly, mayhem broke out. Wholly shocked and terrified by what they'd witnessed, crowds of people at various nearby establishments became an untamed, screaming mob, concerned only with getting away from the scene."

"Two hundred and twenty-five young men on a Boy Scout trip to West Point, New York, are missing. Fifty individuals traveling to Australia through the Leadership Bound Ambassador Program have gone missing."

Another commercial break came on the air with this message: "Take the lead in your community. Strength comes in numbers. We need you to make a real and lasting impact. Do you love your kids? Are you taking care of your aging parents? Do you want to start a new business? Need money for college? Find out how the My Access Chip can help you. Just visit www.myaccesschip.com."

"Another breaking news report," Jenny Purdue announced when she came back on air. "Four police officers were having breakfast at Benny's Bistro in Concord, New Hampshire, when three men and a woman fatally shot them at point-blank range. The perpetrators then escaped to Market Basket on 80 Storey Boulevard and 109 Fort Miles. According to law enforcement officers, they killed five more people, and then themselves, in an outward suicide pact. "

The camera panned over numerous newscasters ranting breathlessly into their microphones.

"We have a report from the actual location now," Jenny Purdue said. "Andrea, tell us what's happened."

"We've learned that a senator, in town for a rally, was possibly in the Market Basket and has been killed."

"Do you know the name of the senator?"

"No," Andrea reported.

A series of camera close-ups revealed people being held back by law enforcement officers. Their faces displayed shock and terror.

A petrified mother was seen dragging her three children in from the boulevard through the front door of an office building.

"I do know that the ambush at Benny's Bistro killed Officers Alberto Reyes, 25, Silvia Stewart, 36, Charlie Harold, 54, and Bryan Williams, 48. All of the officers were pronounced dead at Concord Memorial Hospital. They all leave spouses and children behind. It was reported that one of the killers shouted before killing himself, 'This is a movement! The time is now. The choice is yours.' The Concord Police Department is still investigating the shootings. Once more insight about the shootings is shared, the Chief of Police will hold a press conference," Andrea said.

"We're eagerly awaiting the name of the senator," Jenny Purdue stressed.

"I'll share more information as it becomes available," Andrea assured her.

Another commercial aired: "Beware of the group denouncing the My Access Chip. They don't have your best interest at heart. It's clear they have no intention of working with us to ensure the world is safer, secure, and you have peace of mind. It's their way or the highway, and that's no way to treat YOU! Get chipped today. Visit www.myaccesschip.com."

A camera zoomed in on Jenny Purdue. In a horrified state, she said, "We just learned the name of the senator who was killed. It was Senator Ryan Paul Patrick."

Senators from all over the country had traveled to Concord, New Hampshire for a special meeting to discuss programs focused on empowerment and stability for people who had been impacted by some financial hardship caused by a change in employment status, housing, health issues, transportation, or other matters. The collaboration was intended to help ensure the financial security of this population of people by focusing on protection from financial institutions.

Back in Dallas, Texas, the time for two old friends to reunite had finally come. Mo Money Monte and Bone Esquire sat at Horton's Seafood Restaurant. Bone had invited Mo Money

Monte to an early brunch at one of Dallas' most sophisticated seafood restaurants. It would be Bone's last of many attempts to convince Mo Money Monte to join the movement. Bone thought it would be the perfect place for them to reminisce about their days as sought-after rappers.

"Thank you for meeting me here," Bone said. "Seeing you brings back some good memories of what we accomplished together."

Looking around, Mo Money Monte said, "I see you invited me to some highfalutin restaurant. Where are the rest of the patrons? We could have met at Joe's Fish House."

"Man, I'm getting you ready for the big leagues. My new record label spares no expense when it comes to making sure I'm happy. When you're in the big leagues, an establishment will open its doors early just for you."

In the background, there was a live jazz band with a male vocalist.

"Just look at the beautiful aquariums and oceanic theme throughout the restaurant. The attire of the wait staff. Tuxedo style. No holes like those in the walls of Joe's Fish House. Plus, I'm not parking my 2021 Porsche Panamera on gravel. Only establishments with paved parking lots and valet services for me."

Mo Money Monte sat listening to Bone, a little apprehensive, wondering about his true motive for wanting to meet.

"After today, you could be wearing designer suits made in Italy, like me. As a matter of fact, we can take the company jet to New York and shop at Barney's after we finish eating. The record label has given me access to the jet and secured me an account with no limit," Bone said, staring at Mo Money Monte, who was dressed in a black hoodie and denim jeans.

Dressed in his charcoal two-piece suit, Bone started to discuss a public relations campaign that would reintroduce them to the world.

A waitress appeared, ready to take their drink orders.

"Order anything you want," Bone said to Mo Money Monte. "I remember you being a Crown and Coke man."

"I don't drink alcohol anymore," Mo Money Monte said harshly.

Bone began to laugh and said, "Okay. Sparkling water."

"I'll have a glass of water," Mo Money Monte said, responding to the waitress.

"I'll take a glass of Remy Martin Louis VIII."

"I remember Remy Martin, but what in the world is the 'Louis VIII' part?"

Bone sat smug and said, "It's the top of the line cognac at $175 a glass."

Mo Money Monte simply shook his head in response to Bone's comment.

Bone sat admiring Mo Money Monte's body builder physique and said, "I've really missed you, man."

Pondering what to say, Mo Money Monte stayed quiet.

"You look good. You left us as a tall, lanky something."

Mo Money Monte opened his mouth, hesitated, folded his arms, and continued to glare at Bone.

"My new music is tight. *The Pledge Concert Access Tour* has started and is going great, but the team wants you and me together. They've already gotten us an interview scheduled with a major network, and they added you to the tour schedule. We're positioned to blow up! Nobody will be able to touch us."

Bone was reluctant to share detailed information with Mo Money Monte. Having received information about his newfound religious status, he'd been warned to be cautious about his attempts to woo him over to the movement.

"Wow. All the while I was locked up, you never reached out to me," said Mo Money Monte, disbelieving Bone. "So, how do you just casually say all that? You never once visited me. Now these recent attempts to get with me since my release from prison...why?"

Bone sat, smiling nervously.

"Ugh," Mo Money Monte said, gawking at Bone. "Why now?"

"With the way things went down with your arrest, it complicated things, Mo Money Monte. But you're right, since your release from prison, I've been trying to make this meeting happen," Bone said. "You've ignored my text messages and telephone calls."

The waitress appeared, placing their drinks on the table.

"Thank you. Give us a few minutes to order," Bone said to the waitress.

"Complicated things how? I knew there was some motive behind you wanting to see me, especially after I heard you changed record labels," Mo Money Monte said loudly.

The waitress turned back around, as if Mo Money Monte were speaking to her. Bone motioned for her to continue walking away.

Bone looked around and noticed other wait staff staring at them. "Calm down, man. Calm down. I'm here now. What's more important is that I'm here now. Me, you, and taking over the music world! Once we're back together again, no musician on this planet will be able to match our combined talents."

Mo Money Monte sat, becoming captivated by Bone's arrogance.

Bone started to recoil his arms and placed his hands on the table. "All systems are ready to go, but I must tell you our backers and the producers are worried about your involvement with Pastor McFarland and the fact that you aren't accepting the Chip."

"What?"

"The Chip, Man. The My Access Chip!" Bone extended his hand, palm down.

"How do they know that?" Mo Money Monte frowned. "How do they know about me and Pastor McFarland? And my acceptance or non-acceptance of a Chip?"

"Mo! The Organizers know everything," Bone replied, nodding his head.

"What Organizers?" Mo Money Monte said, getting agitated. "Who are the Organizers?"

"They only reveal themselves to Chip bearers!" Bone leaned his body forward, placed his left elbow on the table, and continued. "Let's focus on the future. We can pick up right where we left off. That is, once you get the Chip."

Bone was heavily trying to get Mo Money Monte to conceive of all of the wonders they could achieve together. The excitement on his face and talk of taking over the music world made Mo Money Monte even more defiant.

"They're relying on us both to help them further the movement. They really don't want anyone to die for not accepting it!"

"There's no picking up where we left off for me," Mo Money Monte announced proudly, with a slight chuckle. "And I'm not helping anyone further something that's against my Christian beliefs."

"Look at this," Bone said. He reached inside his blazer and flashed a wad of money. "There's more where this came from. And you can be driving that Bentley you always talked about and living a life of luxury like me. More than we could have ever imagined back in the day. I'm a part of this group now that's poised to rule the world, and they know they need us to attract a market they can't penetrate alone."

"Did my father set you up to talk with me?" Mo Money Monte asked. "Is this why he's been trying to cozy up to me? Is this why he arranged my release from jail? With all the sudden attention from him and now you, I figured the two of you are conspiring together."

Mo Money Monte wanted to provoke admittance from Bone that he'd joined forces with his dad.

"I don't know anything about your dad, Mo," Bone said.

"His pitch and your pitch sound pretty similar," Mo Money Monte said in disbelief. "His mentioning of Pastor McFarland and the Chip? I know that's not a coincidence."

Bone looked sincerely and said, "I surely don't know what you're talking about."

Mo Money Monte looked disturbed. "It doesn't matter. I'm a different person now. Bentleys and worldly possessions don't excite me. I've turned my life over to God. The hard-core gangster lifestyle and rap music are no longer for me. The only someone I'm following is the Word of God."

"No, you're not different. You're just like me! A gangster!" Bone said loudly. "Forget that Christian mumbo jumbo. That's why you almost got yourself killed in prison."

"What did you say?" snapped Mo Money Monte. "Did someone on the outside have something to do with my stabbings?"

"I don't know anything about your stabbings," Bone said. "I just know the Organizers are ready to position us on a stage that's bigger than you and I could have ever imagined."

"Have you asked yourself why?"

"I know why! Because they know the power of our influence. Our supporters. Our followers. Our fans. Right now, I have three billion followers on my social media forum, iAccessagram."

"What's iAccessagram?" Mo Money Monte asked.

"It's a social networking forum for sharing information about our music products. Showcasing our music videos. Gaining support. Diversifying our audience."

There was an intense silence. The two watched each other, each waiting for the other to say or do something.

After several moments, Mo Money Monte said, "I'm about to release a Christian rap album. I've been working on my music while in prison. I have a Christian producer."

Bone started to laugh uncontrollably. "That's CRAZY! There's no money in that! Who are you gonna attract with Christian rap? You are MO MONEY MONTE. Ain't nobody gonna listen to Christian rap from you! You're a gangster!"

Mo Money Monte replied, "Like I said, money and material things are no longer at the top of my priorities list. I'm doing it because of my love for God and the salvation that comes with serving Him! And I want to let others with a love for rap music know they can still rap, listen to rap, and serve God!"

"Where's your tattoo, Brotherhood A&O Mafia?" Bone took off his blazer and raised the sleeve of his shirt to remind Mo Money Monte of the tattoo they shared. Bone reminded Mo Money Monte why they created Brotherhood Alpha and Omega Mafia. It would be their signature image, symbolizing that they were the beginning and the end, the first and the last.

"I had it removed."

"How did you get so brainwashed in the system?" Bone asked. "Prison is supposed to make you harder."

After talking for a while, it was apparent that neither person would give credence to the other's perspective. They agreed to disagree on what they would do next.

"It's all good, man," Bone said. "The Chip is now mandatory. And if you don't get it by the deadline date, you'll surely die."

With thoughts racing swiftly through his head, Mo Money Monte said softly, "I'll be praying for you, Bone."

"Yeah. You do that. And I'm praying you'll see our position on the Chip and our reconciliation before it's too late for you. Your time for acceptance will run out very soon."

"I'm letting you know now that I'm out." Mo Money Monte scooted back his chair and stood up. "And by the way, I'm going by my birth name, Ivan Shepherd."

"So, you took back the name of the man who's never wanted to have anything to do with you," Bone said smugly. "I'm offering you a family who wants you. Who will give you the world and all you deserve as your name, Mo Money Monte, signifies. I know that pastor you're following is a loser and can't do anything for you, like we can."

"Have you been spying on me? How do you know about my pastor?" Mo Money Monte said.

"Pastor McFarland and his followers will surely die soon for not supporting the movement," Bone said calmly. "I don't wanna see you and those you love in that number."

Standing in his bedroom at seven o'clock on a Wednesday evening, Larry called Mr. Meyers. He knew something serious had happened because his wife, kids, and mother-in-law were gone.

"Hi, Larry, what's going on? I'm having dinner with my family."

"Mr. Meyers, my family is gone."

"What do you mean, gone?"

"I can tell that clothes have been packed and essential items taken."

"What about your wife's car? Is it there?"

"Yes, it's in the driveway."

"They're chipped, right?"

"No, sir."

"What do you mean, no sir? For months, you've known the importance of them being chipped!"

"I know, sir."

"Call Sam immediately, so he can get the team working on their whereabouts. They were there this morning, right?"

"They couldn't have gotten too far."

"You don't know who's helping them."

"Have Sam check out McFarland. He has that domestic violence program. He could be behind their disappearance."

"My wife did mention earlier this year that she listened to him on the radio talking about the chip."

"If you'd demanded she get chipped and had taken matters into your own hands like having Dr. Simon chip everyone in your household at your home, we wouldn't be having this conversation right now. Our entire project is at risk."

"I know, sir."

"That lunatic McFarland has been a thorn in our sides. It's time he be dealt with as well. He thinks he's clever with all his scripture references and the like. He'll see that his so-called God can't stop us, or save him." Mr. Meyers suddenly ended their telephone call.

On the edge of hysteria, Larry called Sam.

"Hey, Larry."

"Sam, I need you to check out McFarland."

"What's going on?"

"I think he's responsible for the disappearance of my wife and kids."

"What do you mean the disappearance of your wife and kids?"

"They're nowhere to be found. Mr. Meyers is afraid my wife may have information to relinquish to McFarland and his people about the chip."

"No worries. Your wife and kids are chipped, right?"

"No, Sam. They're not."

Larry heard a loud gasp on the other end of the telephone line.

"Okay. I'm on it. I'll get a surveillance team on him and all he's closely associated with. I'll get some of my law enforcement contacts to start working their informants and resources. I'll keep you posted."

"I'm afraid this is going to jeopardize my standing with Mr. Meyers, Mr. Denmart, and Natas."

"I'll find them."

Larry sat on the bed, thinking about all he'd invested. He thought, *I should have had the doctor come to our home and chip her, the kids, and her mother. But because I let her have her way, I'm here now, about to lose everything — or worse.*

CHAPTER 10

Bone Esquire stood leaning on the railing of Chasity's balcony, watching the cars traveling below. He was wearing a white T-shirt imprinted with the words *Choice. Change. Access a new and better way of life*, with his designer jeans and Perry Ellis saddles. Chasity came out barefoot, in a satin robe. She placed her arm around his waist and touched his shoulder with her face.

"You okay?" Chasity asked.

"It's about to get really real, Chasity," Bone said.

"The tour is going well, right?" Chasity inquired.

Bone hesitated and said, "Mr. Denmart and Mr. Natas will be in town in a few days."

"I've met them both, and they're pretty cool."

"I presume they're pretty cool as long as things are going their way."

"What do you mean?"

"They're about to make some examples of folks who are refusing the chip."

"And rightfully so," Chasity exclaimed. "I know Pastor McFarland is about to meet his maker, according to my dad."

"The new book by Dr. Irene Cooper has caused pandemonium. A review was released today in the *Dallas Times Newspaper*. Plus, McFarland is having a press conference before the start of his three-day *Wake Call Up* Conference on Friday, and she's a guest speaker."

"No worries. Our executives will draw attention away from his conference. I assure you. What's the title of her new book?"

"*SuperElite: Exercising Global Power.*"

"Interesting title. What's it about?" Chasity asked.

Bone Esquire left to go inside to retrieve a copy of the newspaper. He returned and handed the article to Chasity.

Chasity read the review from the columnist aloud. "A group of elite individuals from all sectors of the world are working diligently behind the scenes to position one person to rule the world. They are leaders in global business, economics, politics, and religion…making and dominating decisions that impact our lives. They move around secretly, thinking we're terribly ignorant of their attempts to position the one designated as the supreme one to gain control over all of us. Don't be swayed by their charm and advocacy of a better life for all. They are self-serving, profit-seeking human piranhas that embody corruption and dominance."

"And I'm afraid for Mo Money Monte. He's heavily connected with these individuals and has become a target. I hear he's speaking, as well, at the conference."

"A target? Again, rightfully so," Chasity reiterated. "You're not going soft on me, are you? Or having second thoughts about the movement?"

"Never."

"Let's focus on your song being number one on the music Billboard charts."

"I just wish Mo Money Monte was experiencing the greatness with me. It's because of him that I'm in music. He believed in me. He taught me everything I know."

"So, maybe that's why God placed him in your life. To get you started. Maybe your time together was only for a season."

◆

Larry Shepherd sat in a small diner in Ennis, Texas, awaiting his companions.

A waitress came to his table and asked, "What can I get you to drink?" as she placed a menu on the table in front of him.

He picked up the menu and glanced at the menu offerings. "I'll have a roast beef sandwich and a cup of coffee."

"Cream and sugar?"

"Yes, thank you."

Moments later, the waitress placed a mug filled with coffee on the table.

"Thank you."

Two glamorous women entered the diner, dressed in beautifully fitted dresses. They walked towards Larry and kissed him on the cheek.

"Hi, sweethearts."

They both smiled at him.

"Dad, are you excited about Sunday?"

Sunday, August 22nd, 2021, he, Mr. Denmart, Mr. Meyers, and Jim Natas had a date to appear at The Kennedy Multicultural Center in South Dallas, Texas. David Denmart, chairman and CEO of Global Media Sources, would stand alongside Jim Natas, the owner of iTrack, as he received *The Washington Post's* Trumpet Award for the My Access Chip device.

Larry looked down at his sandwich and nodded. "Yes, I'm excited. But, right now, I'm more focused on the pre-season football games, jazz festivals, end of summer festivities, and back to school catastrophes we need to finalize. I'm counting on the added efforts of Big Mike and Stanley."

"Have they found Betty, the kids, and her mom yet?"

Larry tilted his head with a grimacing look and said, "Not yet. And that's one conversation I don't want to have with Mr. Meyers on Saturday during our golf game. With the awards ceremony on Sunday and all that's at stake, their lingering disappearance isn't good."

"Later this morning, the *Wake Up Call* conference will kick off. We'll both be in our respective places," Pam assured her father.

"Good. What are you all eating?"

"I'm good, I had a smoothie earlier," Jasmine said.

"I'm good, too."

"I'm so grateful to both of you and the way you've helped Global Media Sources. Jasmine, because of you Pastor Dobbs is performing above and beyond for the movement. His team is posting on social media all throughout the day about getting chipped. And now you've stolen the heart of Jim Natas. Pam, I know you still have some work to do with Mo Money Monte. But after he learns about the disappearance of his mother, you'll be able to persuade him to be a part of the concert and get chipped."

"Yes, Dad, he's a work in progress," Pam said with a smile. "That Pastor McFarland has him brainwashed."

"No worries. We're down to our last option. I'll set things in motion. There will be another disappearance, the one that will surely get his attention."

The waitress appeared with Larry's sandwich.

"Thank you. The food is always incredible here."

The ladies watched Larry as he took a bite of the sandwich.

"Has he tried to be romantic with you?"

"No, Daddy. Probably because he's trying to maintain his religious values."

"Good. I don't need brother and sister kissing and the like," he said with a laugh.

"No worries, Dad."

"I'm proud to say we've reached over five billion implants. But we still have a ways to go."

As with Mo Money Monte, Pam and Jasmine, two non-identical twin sisters, were products of Larry's outside relationships. He hadn't been aware they existed until they researched his whereabouts and contacted him after their stepfather's death five years ago. After the mysterious death of their mother, a long-term mistress of Larry's, their stepfather raised them as his own. Larry cherished his daughters and showered them with expensive gifts. He'd manipulated them into agreeing to keep their existence private. After years of mistreatment by their stepfather, they were willing to do anything to keep their biological father happy. He'd convinced them to help him pull off an elaborate plot to win over preachers, politicians, and Mo Money Monte.

The time had come for Pastor McFarland's *Wake Up Call* conference. He and his supporters were excited about having a huge forum for presenting their case against getting chipped.

In front of the cameras on the steps of Triumphant Baptist Church, he stated, "Christians of all denominations are being misled. A device that will alter the minds and characters of all generations is being promoted as your way to a better life. The promoters of the device are using politicians, celebrities, sports figures, and even clergy to gain support and enthusiasm for their chip. In turn, they're receiving private donations to persuade you that it's all good."

A reporter spoke out, "Who are they?"

"There's a group out there affiliated with Global Media Sources and iTrack, Inc., promoting an implantable chip. I'm sure many of you are seeing the infomercials, billboard advertisements, and magazine and TV interviews. Scripture in the Bible talks about the Antichrist, who will make all have a character in his or her right hand or on his or her forehead. What we're seeing is prophecy being revealed. You're seeing more and more messages about this implantable chip. Its promoters started saying its purpose was for identification purposes for the sick and elderly. That it would contain vital health information needed in an emergency. But there's a bigger agenda. *New World Access.* They're going to great lengths to force people to get chipped. Remember the trash can bombings, the plane crashes, the shooting of Senator Ryan Paul Patrick, four police officers, and others who were killed."

Another reporter spoke loudly, "Those are some pretty strong accusations, Pastor McFarland."

"Yes, I know they are. But they're true. They're pulling out a number of tactics to instill both fear and necessity."

"I saw a billboard on Highway 360 that said, 'Receiving some sort of government assistance? Then it's time to change your status from un-chipped to chipped. Continuance of your services depends it. Visit www.myaccesschip.com for a location near you. Getting chipped means easy access to your benefits. Food stamps. Unemployment Benefits. Medicare. Social Security. Housing. Medicaid. Veteran Services. Thinking you have time? NO, you don't! Don't delay. Get chipped today,'" a lady said.

Another reporter shouted out, "What's your take on *New World Access*?"

"One government. One religion. One monetary system. It's biblical. There's a theme with a framework of accepting the chosen one's system of oneness. For the true believers who understand the Rapture, we know Jesus is coming back soon. He'll descend from heaven and take His brides, those who are born-again Christians, and take them up into heaven to be with Him in His kingdom. Disappearing to all of those who are left behind."

A reporter asked, "What will happen to those left behind?"

Pastor McFarland recognized the reporter as Jasmine Walker.

"It's good to see you, Ms. Walker."

Jasmine smiled.

"Especially considering your employer."

"I'm capturing all perspectives, Pastor McFarland."

Pastor McFarland smiled back and said, "Those left behind will remain on Earth and suffer to the end of the Tribulation."

There was heightened chatter among many of those listening to the press conference.

"The conference will be starting in an hour. We're excited about our speakers, Political Consultant Irene Cooper, Christian Rapper and Producer Ivan Shepherd, Financial Mogul Trey McDonald, and many more. To hear me expound on the Rapture and the Tribulation, I invite everyone to come to our Wednesday night Bible study. I've been teaching on the subjects for the past couple of years."

The start of the conference was underway, and people from all walks of life were in attendance.

Pastor McFarland started off with a prayer, "Lord, I thank You for the opportunity to be here today. I thank You for the opportunity to share, educate, and encourage those in attendance to continue to follow the biblical word You've given us."

The invited speakers spoke to the audience one by one.

Trey McDonald said, "Rev. McFarland is the theologian. I only understand, based on my readings, without the Mark, no one will be able to buy or sell. Doesn't that sound like what's coming? First, they said the implantable chip would be used for identification purposes. Now, it's being forced on us. Those who are receiving government services must have the chip. In order to purchase certain products, you must have the chip. Starting now, I'm recommending that everyone implement their plan to become debt-free. Start making your purchases, at least minor ones like food, gas, clothing, with cash. Let's lessen their ability to track us and what we're doing and where we're spending our money. To say we need the chip to make purchases is the ultimate control. Don't let these TV commercials convince you that the chip is the way to go."

Mo Money Monte, under his birth name, said, "What they're trying to force on us should anger any true believer, but it's prophecy being fulfilled. Just like the death of Jesus Christ. Those free concerts making headlines now are designed to bribe our young folks to get chipped. Millions of dollars are being spent by those who want the Chip to control the world and all that's in it. Whether they like it or not, they're gonna lose in the end. We're gonna beat them through individualized chats, helping people get the facts about the chip, and pulling apart the lies their supporters are spreading about the chip and its benefits. We can circumvent their efforts because we have a higher, stronger, and smarter force than just a heap of money. We'll never be able to match up with their checkbook - and we don't need to, because we have a much more influential tool in the hundreds of thousands of Christians standing against the chip."

People began to clap. He glanced over at his mother and smiled.

Dr. Irene Cooper walked up to the podium. "In my new book, *SuperElite*, I cover a lot of territory. We're against this sort of device and the level of control it's designed to have."

"Speak the truth, Dr. Cooper!" someone yelled from the crowd.

She continued, "Invasion of privacy. Who wants to have their every move detected and recorded? They're trying to make it seem like it's all for our benefit, but it's not. Don't be fooled by their tricky words of safety. As the speakers before me have said,

I assure you that this is all biblical prophecy. The Antichrist's Mark of the Beast. They have these entertainers now trying to sway your kids and young people. Read your Bibles, the Book of Revelation."

To conclude the conference, Pastor McFarland came up to the podium. "As the speakers have all echoed, please don't be fooled by their trickery. The implantable chip has been created to bring into action a higher plan to implement a system that will enable the chosen one to control us through one government, one religion, and one financial system. To track and control all of us, from the loaf of bread or package of toilet paper we buy, to the dinner we purchase while on vacation in London, to our private time of reading scriptures in the Bible, to watching our favorite show on television."

Pastor McFarland looked out into the audience with peace and contentment.

"Don't worry. Those of us who are true believers will not be here much longer. We're on our way to be with the Most High. Until that happens, don't accept their Pledge, and don't get chipped. I want to remind all of us to keep this scripture from Revelation, chapter nineteen, verse twenty, in plain sight: 'Then the beast was captured, and with him the false prophet who worked signs in his presence, by which he deceived those who received the mark of the beast and those who worshiped his image. These two were cast alive into the lake of fire burning with brimstone.'" (Revelation 19:20 NKJV)

Pastor McFarland paused.

"The choice to accept or reject the implantable chip, our modern day beast, will be your greatest test. No one is exempt from facing the choice. If you choose the chip, you'll suffer the wrath of God. If you refuse the chip, you'll receive His favor."

www.ingramcontent.com/pod-product-compliance
Lightning Source LLC
Chambersburg PA
CBHW032030050726
47590CB00006B/2367